ADVANCE PRAISE

The Wave tells us how to create a future in which creativity, empathy, and social imagination are the primary forces in our daily lives. Everything in it is doable and practical. It is a road map to the future country we want to live in.

—Gloria Steinem

If we're going to end this fiscal madness and start rebuilding America, we're going to have to get creative! We need a tsunami of music, film, poetry and art. *The Wave* is about changing the story to change the world. Buy it, read it, share it!

—Van Jones, Rebuild The Dream

Reading *The Wave* feels like riding The Wave—you catch its power and delight in its natural force, as it supports you right up onto the beach of the future. Its vision is one you always had in you, but didn't quite know it was there. It taps more than hope, it activates a kind of knowing, writ loud and clear, so we all can see what could be. It is as empowering as an activist's handbook as it ʲ ative for entrepreneurs. Arlene Goldbard evinces wh k, and what can answer the dilemmas that ʳ ə has sharpened my vision, reframed ʲhat comes after Occupy. *The Wave* y yin to the yang of *The Culture of Possib.*

—Eric Booth, educator, ɑ ɔ advisor to El Sistema

These days, in the Horrific Triumph of Capitalism, it seems that Hope is a Thing called Pleather. To bust these blinders, go RIGHT NOW to the rocking vision of Arlene Goldbard, a revolutionary armed with art and joy, treatises for the imagination. Her argument is—there's No Argument! Live Art! Her writing links to songs we can dance to—what happens if the theory is a poem? Being interactive for her is a thing called Community—a Community for all Humanity. You discover yes, there is a New Consciousness, and it ain't no digital alienation. It's a way of living that puts the juice in, and the jazz, and the genuine. All this in a book? Open it up, and you'll open up too.

—Bob Holman, poet, founder, Bowery Poetry Club

THE WAVE

THE WAVE

ARLENE GOLDBARD

Arlene Goldbard

To Steve,
In friendship,
Arlene

The Wave
Arlene Goldbard
Waterlight Press
www.thewavenovel.com

Library of Congress Control Number: 2013937646
ISBN-10 0989166902
ISBN-13 978-0989166904

CONTENTS

INTRODUCTION

The Wave was written to answer a question I am often asked: *You say that we are on the cusp of a paradigm shift, a radical change in worldview that will thrust art and culture onto center stage. What does that mean? How will the world be different?*

The Wave is speculative fiction. In 2023, a young journalist, Rebecca Price, writes a series of articles describing an emergent cultural change that has been gathering force over the previous decade (even longer, some of her informants say). She draws on a range of examples unfolding in New York City, where she lives. "The Wave," her name for the *Zeitgeist*—the rising spirit of the times—catches on, entering common usage. In 2033, she is asked by an editor to revisit her findings and report again. The text includes notes to her editor, excerpts from the 2023 series, and new material she writes in 2033.

Who can know how the future will unfold? I claim no predictive powers. But I have been careful not to include anything in *The Wave* that could not be enacted in the next twenty years. My hope is that a glimpse of this possible world will spark other social imaginations, and that readers will be inspired to add to our collective dream of a future worth pursuing, one that can override the dystopian self-discouragement that has become our daily fare.

Special thanks to Sharon De La Peña Davenport, Adam Horowitz, and Tom Mandel for their help, to Martha Richards, Executive Director of WomenArts, and the Nathan Cummings Foundation for their generous support during the creation of this book, and to all the artists and activists whose work inspires me.

Arlene Goldbard

Richmond, California

PREVIEW:
A GLIMPSE OF
THE GREAT CONVERSATION
NEW YORK CITY, 2023

"Lulu can speak for herself, of course," Rebecca said as she scanned their faces. "But she's already raised the question of whether The Wave is just another luxury masquerading as social change, like the Prius a couple of decades ago. What do you think?"

Lisa was the first to speak. "I don't think any social phenomenon has just one meaning. Yes, the Prius was a way for people with money to feel better about driving. It also cut carbon emissions. The fact that everyone couldn't afford one didn't cancel the fact that it was an improvement over gas-guzzlers. It paved the way for hybrid cars, electric cars, hydrogen-fueled cars, and much better car-sharing and public transit. It was both, a luxury and a harbinger."

"'The perfect is the enemy of the good,'" said Anya. "If I had a dollar for every time I've quoted Voltaire on that one, I'd be a rich woman, my dears. That was a kind of left-wing malady when I was young: reject everything that fails to meet your standards of perfection, and always be harder on anything that tries."

"That's not fair!" said Lulu. "Pretending to do good when you're only exploiting an issue for profit can be worse, because you're fooling people into thinking they're making things better."

"Worse? That's a tough question," Anya replied. "What are you measuring? If you're measuring actual carbon footprint, then reducing it a little is better than not reducing it at all. If you're measuring hypocrisy, then yes, it's more hypocritical. Hypocrisy is bad, I give you that. But no one dies of it. It's actions that kill, not attitudes."

"Attitudes lead to actions," Lulu retorted. "Let's say someone could have spent their time working for better public transit, or an end to fossil fuels, but instead that person fell for the Prius propaganda and felt all righteous about it. Those are actions, right? Actions that didn't happen and had real consequences."

"Sure," said Will. "But every time you do X instead of Y, there are consequences of some kind. What is at stake in this argument? How does it matter if Anya wins or Lulu wins?"

"Ah," said Jacob, "a realist in our midst. Everything matters to Lulu," he said, extending a hand to take one of hers, "that is who she is. But yes. This thing Rebecca is calling 'The Wave' is many things at once, I think. A luxury, a necessity. An image, a reality...."

TO: ED LUPO, ZEITGEIST.COM

25 May 2033

Hi, Ed:

As I ponder this juicy assignment you've given me, I've been thinking of a quotation I first used as an email signature back in college. (I actually used it again to start off the final section of "Chronicles of The Wave" in 2023.) I got it from an English professor who credited the poet Randall Jarrell. "The people who live in a Golden Age," Jarrell wrote, "usually go around complaining how yellow everything looks." I thought then that he nailed it, and I think it still. I kvetch, therefore I am—that ought to be our species' motto.

It occurs to me that we human beings like reality neatly packaged: *La Belle Epoque*, the Renaissance, the Middle Ages. My little contribution: "The Wave." But in the here and now, reality rarely yields so easily to branding. It isn't as if the people who inhabited these eras came pre-labeled. Like us, they just lived their lives, paddling along the stream of time. But later, when someone came up with the right verbal container for a parcel of the past—a label with the right stickiness—that was that.

My grandfather once told me that he thought of "The Sixties" in capital letters. In his mind's eye, the letters looked psychedelic, like one of those Fillmore posters that became such a big deal to collect a few years ago. He said that he sees all other decades in ordinary numbers. (We were getting stoned together at the time, so take that with a grain of something.) I don't think Grandpa was exaggerating, though, because when he and his codger friends used to get to reminiscing, you could almost see the swirling colors. One of them would say something about "Sixties people," and everyone else would nod sagely, seeming to comprehend all that tag implies.

I am sitting here thinking about the randomness of it all: you asked me to do this retrospective piece because I got lucky with "The Wave," and that label stuck. Now, everybody says it: "What was it like when The Wave started, Daddy?" "I came up in The Wave, so of course I like that kind of music." But it isn't as if on day one—some time in 2013, say—the earth moved and everything changed. While it was all unfolding, most people still thought the future was going to resemble the ultimate disaster movie. God knows we were already seeing the previews, already complaining about how extremely yellow everything looked.

Still, I understand why you asked me to do this ten-year look back at my first Wave piece. "Chronicles of The Wave" more or less made me as a writer, so I feel I owe it something, if that makes sense. But despite the temptation to deliver a tidy, polished argument for the inevitability of what has already happened, I don't want to sand the rough edges off my account of those days. So let's just call it *meta*, okay? I've bitten off hunks of my 2023 narrative for your edification: that's the stuff in Arial, the typeface of the era. In the spaces between, I've include anything that hindsight suggests (Times Roman of course; always a traditionalist at heart). Let's talk about it whenever you're ready.

Cheers,

Rebecca

CATCHING THE WAVE

by Rebecca Price

2033

It all started because I was pissed off at my parents. They always knew just how to get to me, and I always got hooked—and that always made my blood boil. One night I was so down on myself for getting triggered, I couldn't fall asleep. I lay in bed staring at the moon-shadows on the rumpled quilt. I felt as if my body were made of knotted rope. In short, I was beating the shit out of myself: if maturity was letting your parents' nagging wash over you without leaving stains, I told myself, I was like some toddler festooned with half my dinner.

I kept mentally replaying that night's Skype conversation with Mom and Dad. Perched side-by-side on the couch, the parents looked a little blurry. I thought it was less a tech problem than the agitation they felt around the subject of my dubious career. Which is why I never ever brought up the subject (and obviously, why they always did).

My brother Ben—four years younger—had just been promoted to some even more prestigious and better-paying job at the new-tech computer corp that had employed him since graduation. He had a house and a dog and even a girlfriend (whom my mother would only describe as "very nice, very intelligent," which I mentally translated into "another geek, dear, a member of his own tribe"). So that was the cue for my Dad to mention that there were writing jobs there too, back home in California, with enlightened employers who laid on free shuttles and free healthy-gourmet lunches, not to mention an abundance of Ben's nice single male friends. And that was my cue to lose it, first yelling at them for not respecting my choices, then biting my tongue instead of asking for another loan, which is what I'd planned to do.

I had no way to explain what I was feeling in those days. I thought it was all too vague and touchie-feelie for them to understand. I was moving through my life with the feeling that something big was taking shape, a story that I was uniquely suited to tell. I had the idea that it just needed a little bit more time to come into focus. Except that sounded pretty grandiose, even inside my own head. So I kept playing a kind of mental ping-pong with myself: I'd get all glowy with the vast possibility of it all, and then look in the mirror and ask myself what special qualities could be claimed by a 29 and 1/2 year-old creative writing graduate who'd been freelancing for not quite eight New York years without making much of an impression?

I'd count up my assets, whistling in the dark. I knew I was relentless, an advantage for a writer. I knew I was a pretty good writer too, getting better all the time. But I didn't know for sure what I wanted to write *about*. I was nagged by this feeling that the texture of reality had altered, that it had taken on a new shape, and that my ability to see patterns in seemingly disparate things was helping me to perceive its true meanings. I just wasn't quite ready to say what they were. I thought that my parents probably would have had me committed if they'd heard me say that, so I didn't. I just felt this intense sense of becoming, permanent butterflies.

I managed to fall asleep eventually. Less than twenty-four hours later, I had an idea courtesy of my roommate Lulu. She was part of the storyteller corps at Bellevue, an excellent gig: good pay, nice people, endless interesting stories. She'd usually come home after a day at the hospital ready to spin out some tale I could barely believe. Lulu had to change the names, of course, and occasionally leave out some little detail. "There's such a thing as medical confidentiality, you know" she would say, adding a little lift of the eyebrows. Some of her stories left me laughing until my stomach ached. Some tore me up.

That evening, to distract me from ranting on about my parents, Lulu acted out the story of an Iranian with heart trouble. He was an old man now, but he'd come into this country as a youngish literature professor and somehow spent the rest of his days filling cups and cleaning tables at a coffee shop on Third Avenue.

Lulu's job was to engage each patient as a person, giving the individual behind the illness plenty of space and encouragement to emerge. She always said you had to understand the realities of people's lives if you were going to help them: what were they living for? What were they up against? What did they think and feel about the disease process occupying their bodies? Which sides were their spirits on: resistance, passivity, forbearance, anger? In the contest with illness, which parts of the person were allied with healing?

Over her four years at Bellevue, Lulu had developed a technique. She usually started with simple queries about the patient's life and feelings, easy ones at first, then moving on to questions that risked touching tender spots. "What was it like to leave everything familiar behind?" she eventually asked the man. To enter a completely new world, she was thinking, to fall so far in social status? "You must have felt discouraged," was what she said.

"I did not have the luxury of feeling that way," the man told her. "My family depended on me. It was my fault we had to leave Teheran. I was young and proud. I knew that we were right about democracy. I could not stop myself saying what I knew, and because of that, I had to come home one night and tell everyone to pack up their things, that we were leaving, maybe forever. It was not until I saw how scared my wife looked that I tasted doubt. By then there was no turning back. Did I do the right thing? Who can judge? All I could know is this: I spoke the truth, and my family paid a very high price."

That evening Lulu told me she'd been impressed by this man, he was so honest about himself. His smile was ironic, his eyes clear and pained. "Would I have done the same if I knew that in this country I would spend most of my life lying in other ways?" he asked. "'Yes, sir,' 'No, sir,' always careful not to disturb anyone with my foreignness? That was the first thing I learned," he told her. "To forget who I thought I was, and to be who I was supposed to be. I did what I had to do to survive. But always, I remember."

"Then he said he'd been in Bellevue before," Lulu told me, her black eyes shining with excitement. "It wasn't long after they immigrated here in the eighties. A cop picked him up: he was disoriented, dizzy. He'd been overcome with nausea and vomited into a trashcan in one of those little median strips on upper Broadway—you know, the ones with two or three benches. He couldn't answer the cop's questions—who is President of the United States, they asked him—so they checked him in for observation. He tried to tell them he was a professor, but that made things worse. How could this messy, incoherent, foreign person be a professor? They poked at him and did some tests. They talked about him as if he weren't there. And every minute he got more frantic about his family. They would be searching for him. They would be scared. They spoke very little English. There was no one else to look after them."

One thing that made Lulu a great storyteller was how completely she empathized with her protagonist. Her eyes swam with fear; her mouth trembled. She had a great mop of black curls, and even her hair seemed distraught. Her hands stayed in the air, sketching the scene.

"Finally," she told me, "someone happened to walk by who could speak a little Farsi, and they recognized a few words he was saying. They took his blood pressure, made sure he was hydrated. His pressure dropped, he calmed down, and they let him go. After he told me about that, he said the most interesting thing to me," Lulu explained. "He said, 'Here you are, ready to listen to me, to make me feel like a human being, instead of a problem in the body of a person. But back then, no one wants to know my story. Not a single person. I think things have changed.'"

Right then, gears started clicking in my head.

"For a minute, I saw the hospital through his eyes," Lulu said. She described it: someone from the storyteller corps sat with every family in the waiting room. On the wards, artists were helping people put their experiences and feelings into images, making collages or digital stories that helped to anchor each person in his or her own healing. Writers were finding words for feelings that otherwise threatened to overwhelm patients. Musicians had their heads bent over hospital beds, collaborating on playlists attuned to whatever each person needed. Patients were teaching musicians the lullabies they'd heard as children.

Hospitals were always busy places: everyone had a job to do, things had to be organized and efficient if there was any hope of responding to the scale of need. But looking through this man's eyes, Lulu had seen freshly what a huge change had taken place: needs were no longer perceived as purely physical, as a simple matter of drawing blood or taking X-rays or palpating organs. To treat disease, everybody knew, they also had to understand it. Disease was a relationship between a human being and an invader, whether that was a virus or bacterium, cells gone haywire, or an oncoming bullet. Healing needed the cooperation of all parties, but they couldn't even be known unless they were invited and engaged. It was just that simple. Through the Iranian man's eyes, Lulu realized that what seemed completely self-evident, practical— normal—to us now would have sounded like a lot of woo-woo crap a generation earlier.

"Everybody talks about how things have changed," Lulu said, "but we kind of take it for granted, too. Think about it, Rebecca!" She grasped me by the arm, pinned me with her eyes. "Just think back a couple of decades: all those people in pain, in trouble, finding themselves in the hospital, almost no one pays any attention to who they *are*, they're just a collection of numbers and symptoms. People want them to heal, there is kindness and compassion—sure. But then they talk about patients like objects, they prescribe pills and order injections without explaining, the patients are scared, and the fear makes everything worse. It all feeds on itself, and each misstep compounds the next, and in some ways, even the people who get better are spit out feeling worse. And this is just the normal way of things in those days. Modern medicine." Lulu shuddered to think about it.

"It made me realize that I have only the vaguest idea of *how* things changed," she said. "Like what was the process? What started it? Where did the change come from? I mean, you could say it came from people getting fed up with the way things were: you know, like this is intolerable and it has to change *right now*. So on one day, change must not have seemed possible, and on the next day, it was just like: oh yeah, new ballgame, let's go with it? I don't get it. What tipped things over?"

We both got excited. We kept talking about it while we foraged in the kitchen for something to eat. The more we talked, the more I felt that vague sense that I'd been having beginning to cohere into some kind of shape. I got a mental image of a wave, like one of those beautiful Hokusai prints, as if the tide had come in and washed away the past. All the old fixed ideas were written on sand. And something big was being inscribed in their place.

I'd been freelancing for a few different sites and apps, and the editors seemed happy enough with my work. But life was pretty marginal. New York was expensive. I wanted to know that I had my share of the rent in the bank every month. I thought I might like something other than ramen for dinner once in a while. Lulu was right: something needed to be named. You heard people talk all the time about how things had changed, but if you asked most people what that was about and how it had come to be, they'd shrug.

I saw my opportunity. It was human to take social arrangements for granted, almost as something given or natural like rocks and trees. Everybody did it. But they weren't natural. They weren't even given. People made them. We needed to remember that. It made people more conscious of having choices, and that was a good thing. It rhymed with my personal psychology, that's for sure: the one thing I'd always known is that I never wanted to feel trapped. We always have choice, I'd tell myself and anyone who'd listen, even if it was a choice of how to respond to the inevitable.

I decided to query my editor at Zeitgeist.com in the morning. I was pretty sure he'd like the story. I even had a working title ready: "Chronicles of The Wave."

CHRONICLES OF THE WAVE
PART 1:
DOCTOR FEELGOOD'S ORIGIN STORY
2023

There was a Doctor Feelgood's store—the flagship—right downstairs from corporate headquarters on Broadway. I timed my arrival for an hour before my interview with Dan Kahn, Doctor Feelgood's founder and CEO. The previous morning, I'd gone online to put my name in the queue for a half-hour with a Virtuoso. It was funny how that word has morphed, I thought, just the way *Genius* hadn't always meant a helpful geek at the Apple store.

Walking through the jade-green door usually triggered a flashback of my first visit way back in 2013, when I was still in college and Dr. Feelgood's was the new-new thing. My friend Annie hadn't been able to stop talking about the place. Despite resisting anything wildly popular (to this day, I still haven't read the Harry Potter books), when Annie offered to treat me to coffee as a bribe, I said yes, figuring that Doctor Feelgood's was right on the way to our favorite coffee place—the one that made the best version of that ultra-slow drip Japanese coffee.

The first ten minutes of that visit, I felt skeptical. I acted polite, adopting the best-behavior attitude appropriate to accompanying someone's grandmother to church. But then a Virtuoso approached, a hip-seeming, friendly woman whose smile had a hint of reserve. "How can I help you today?" she asked.

I shrugged, clueless.

"Have you ever been here before?" The Virtuoso explained that a brief consultation was free for all first-time visitors. She motioned me into a room filled with comfortable-looking chairs and couches. "The idea," she explained, "is to begin talking about anything that needs attention in your life, especially anything that leaves you feeling a little uneasy or off-center. I'll ask you questions, but you don't have to answer unless you want to. After we've talked for a bit, I'll suggest something that might help. You don't have to take my advice, of course, but something interesting could happen if you do."

I thought briefly about bolting, but I was curious. My mouth seemed to open of its own accord. I began to talk about an old friend—not Annie, I'd met her at college. It was Jessica, who'd been my best friend in high school and who somehow didn't fit, didn't mesh anymore with the person I wanted to be. Jessica kept tagging along. It wasn't terrible or anything, but slightly off-key, something like scenes from an old movie being spliced into a very different new one.

The Virtuoso—her name was Mona—listened patiently, then asked if I had ever heard Leonard Cohen's music. A little, I said. My mother loved him. While we were sitting there, Mona texted me the names of two tracks from an old recording called *Ten New Songs*: "Alexandra Leaving," and "Love Itself." "Sit quietly in a room with low lights—or no light at all," Mona said. "Don't do anything except listen to the songs. As you listen, let an image of Jessica linger in your mind. You don't have to think about her or figure anything out. Just let the songs work on you, and pay attention to whatever comes up."

It turned out that those two songs—the whole recording, really—were about loss as an inevitable part of life. Love comes and goes. Everything comes and goes: that's how life works. I listened a half-dozen times, just as Mona had instructed. The experience of just *being* with music, not as a backdrop to life, but as the thing you were doing in and of itself—that was both a reminder and a revelation that had been worth the first visit to Doctor Feelgood's. But there had been more. It was impossible to say precisely how, but the music took the edge off the tension around Jessica. Jessica had new friends too, I realized. She wasn't counting on me to rescue her. When I saw Jessica after that, I didn't need to say or do anything. When I paid attention the way Mona had said to, I was aware of watching things change, of feeling gratitude for the friendship we'd shared, of having that be enough. I knew the music had something to do with it, but exactly what, I couldn't say.

I went back again when something got in the way of what I thought of as the "energy flow" between my boyfriend and myself in senior year. The music was completely different that time: these long, juicy guitar songs packed with a certain erotic flavor, the concentrated essence of longing. "Maggot Brain," which started me listening to Eddie Hazel; "The Beggar" by Mos Def before he became Yasin Bey. I still love that playlist. When my grandmother died—the arty one—it wasn't music at all, but a weeklong festival of the films she saw as a young woman, the classics that almost nobody outside of film studies watched anymore: *Black Orpheus, Jules et Jim, The Battle of Algiers, The Apu Trilogy, Wild Strawberries, Rashomon*....

That had been my first time at Doctor Feelgood's. Now, visiting a decade later (for probably the fiftieth time), I had to shake my head to clear the fog of memory. I looked around the waiting room, trying to see it freshly. There was a hot spot in my stomach, half anxiety and half excitement: I was here on an important story, after all. Even so, it was always a fun place to visit. The front of the store was like a very special museum gift shop.

The seating area was surrounded by interactive kiosks. You could put on headphones and sample playlists sorted by time and circumstance ("Ivy League pre-finals anxiety," read one; "Little sister's wedding shower," read another). You could go into a scent booth to sample moods and memories: plumeria blossoms on a hot island afternoon; a glass of *moscato amabile* under almond trees in blossom. If that made you hungry, there were tiny bites of maximum theobromine chocolate or a kind of soft cheese that smelled like new-mown hay. While you nibbled, you could browse the first few pages of novels and stories categorized by the desires they promised to fulfill: laughter, consolation, arousal, serenity....

Some people used Doctor Feelgood's as a kind of sensory boutique—I could see the fun in that. There was the usual scanner at the door: if your card was synced and you were in a hurry, you could breeze on through, collecting purchases, then breeze out again without interacting with an actual human being. But since my first visit, I'd hardly bought more than a snack there without consulting a Virtuoso. With so much to draw on, it just felt better to have a guide.

As if summoned by that thought, my personal Virtuoso appeared, extending her hand. Paula—tall, upright, graceful, African American, probably late fifties—wore her grey hair in a sort of Virginia Woolf do, coiled into a knot at the back of her neck. She led the way to her consulting room, which looked like the lair of a very hip therapist: not so many Turkish carpets and carvings as I'd seen in the old photos of Freud's professional domain. Instead, shades of green were layered, giving the feeling of dappled sunshine drifting through leaves.

Often, Virtuoso sessions were personal, even intimate. But on this day, I decided not to go into too much detail. I was worried about getting snagged on some corporate p.r. policy if I let Paula know that today's visit was preparation for an interview with Doctor Feelgood's founder. So I just said I had an important meeting in less than an hour and needed help with anxiety. That was true. Paula knew me, she'd already accessed my records to refresh her memory, so she didn't need to ask many questions. She bent briefly over her keyboard, and then the wall was filled with an image of buildings, whole and broken, drenched in setting sunlight. "Corot," said Paula, "sadly neglected, I think. This is his view of the Roman forum from the Farnese Gardens."

"Let yourself feel the light," Paula instructed. "Imagine yourself standing exactly where Corot painted this image, gazing out at the city exactly as it was in the 19th century." I began to sink into a reverie, feeling warm sun on bare arms. The onscreen image faded, gradually replaced by a very different landscape. "Avignon Seen from Villeneuve les Avignon," said Paula.

For the next quarter-hour, one color-saturated landscape followed another. With each image, something seemed to open, an awareness that the enduring beauty of the world was mine to receive, that I was a fit receptacle for the knowledge of it. By the time I left, my breath came slow and deep.

CATCHING THE WAVE,
CONTINUED
2033

It's been a decade, but I can still tune into my feelings that morning. I was high-strung at the best of times; that day, I probably would have spontaneously combusted without that Virtuoso session. When I entered his office, Kahn was fiddling with a tiny recorder on his desk. He wanted to be quoted accurately, no doubt. I wanted the same, but he was so much more powerful, such a public figure, that the sight of the recorder was somehow disconcerting—even though I pulled out my own recorder, of course, impersonating professionalism.

I suppose I felt intimidated in direct proportion to my desire for success. If the profile turned out to be as good as I hoped, I was sure my editor would greenlight the full series, and that would lead to paying the rent on a regular basis. And if I blew it, that would make my parents right forever. I took a deep breath, flashed on Corot, told myself I could ask Kahn anything as long as I was polite—and also that this could be my one and only chance to talk to him, so I should ask him *everything*.

He turned out to be astoundingly forthcoming. He told me all sorts of intimate stuff about his late wife Nikki and the crisis of her death. Dan told me later—he and I became friends after the piece ran—that something about me reminded him of Nikki when they first met. So that was random luck: if I hadn't looked younger than I was—and if I hadn't known how to work that to get an interview subject on my side—who knows if I would have learned as much?

A few weeks later I shared the Dr. Feelgood's part of my text with Dan before publication. My reasoning was this: it wasn't a "gotcha" story, I had a good feeling about him, and I wanted the portrait to feel fair. Still, when I clicked "send," I was nervous. There was a good chance he'd want changes.

Looking back, I'm surprised I felt even as confident as I did, considering that parts of the piece gave the impression that I was narrating Dan's innermost thoughts. I don't think I realized how risky that was. But in the event, he let it stand with almost no changes. That gave me courage to be just as forthcoming with everyone else I interviewed. Later on, I saw that experience as part of The Wave too, having to cope with a lot less need to pretend, to be self-important, to wear the masks, than in the bad old days when CEOs were expected to keep their feelings to themselves (unless they swelled with pride, aggression, patriotism, or "family values") and journalists kept their agendas hidden. Lulu was always talking about "the realness factor." The conversation with Dan Kahn felt real—to both of us.

CHRONICLES OF THE WAVE
PART 1: DOCTOR FEELGOOD'S ORIGIN STORY, CONTINUED
2023

"'Doctor Feelgood?' No, no. I did *not* choose that name." Dan Kahn rubbed his hand over his eyes, then scrubbed distractedly at his neatly trimmed brown goatee. "I resisted it forever, in fact. It sounded like a drug dealer," Kahn explained, "or some kind of sleazy sex guru. And then they started to call me 'Doc,' and I thought, 'Surrender, man: your nickname just got a nickname. You've been branded."

I thought that Kahn looked a little like my father, if my father had been hip rather than hearty: the same average height, average build, brown hair, brown eyes. But Kahn had a beard, and all of his features were held in some kind of loose equilibrium that made me see the outlines of this man at twenty, slouching on a couch draped in Indian bedspreads. His nose and mouth were fleshy, mobile, restless. Back in the day he probably had a joint in one hand and a girl in the other, I guessed. He seemed comfortable in his skin, and that was an appealing quality.

Kahn gestured at the wall behind his desk, a mosaic of framed cartoons and autographed celebrity photos. (*"To Doc, Thanks for the tunes, Steve Jobs."*) A row of colorful labels depicted a cheerful figure with a stethoscope in his ears, the device's bell emitting musical notes.

"The best ideas are thrust upon you?" I asked.

"Damned if I know," Kahn shrugged. "Who can say how the best ideas emerge? But this was one of those force-of-nature things. I decided not to fight it."

"So the name took hold after you opened the business? What did you call it when you started? What came before 'Doctor Feelgood?'"

"Just Dan's," he said.

"Like a diner or something? 'Eat at Dan's?'"

"No, both words: 'Just Dan's.' A little self-effacing, I admit. But that was the mood in 2010. I had a friend in the restaurant business who almost talked me into going with no name, like one of those ultra-hip joints in the old meatpacking district where you had to know the secret door to get in. But then I figured I'd probably go broke that way. I said, 'Okay, what about just Dan's, then?' I was thinking like you were, Dan's, Dan's place or whatever. But my friend made a joke about my well-developed sense of justice, like it was a boast or something: 'Righteous Dan's.' 'Just Dan's.' Somehow it seemed modest *and* arrogant: I went with it."

"Okay," I said. "Take me back there, twelve years ago. How did you get started in 2010?"

Kahn pulled a phone out of his pocket and glanced at it, looking a little impatient. "I'm sure you've read all the press stuff, so the whole creation saga, you must know it inside out by now. What are you looking for?"

"Things have changed a lot since 2010, Mr. Kahn."

"Dan."

"Like I said, I'm doing a series on the cultural change of the last decade. I'm calling it 'The Wave'—whatever the paradigm shift has been that enabled a business like yours to succeed, it seems significant. I don't think any one person made The Wave happen, but your role seems notable; some say catalytic. I've heard the basic story: you know, this happened and then that happened. But it's much bigger than

Doctor Feelgood's, and I still don't understand what really started it all. I thought you might be able to help me."

"This will take coffee," said Dan, lifting the phone to his ear. When he put it down again, he ran his hand through his hair and smoothed the front of his dark blue shirt, as if he were preparing to go onstage. On an out-breath, the corners of his mouth turned down, he said this: "My part of this story started with a loss, a big, big, huge fucking loss."

Even after all this time, Dan didn't love going back there, 2009, Nikki before the end. They'd been happy, he now saw. But at the time—sad, mad, glad, whatever—he never put a name on it. They just were. They'd been together for more than twenty years: "DanandNikki," people said, as if it were one name. He loved her cooking and the smooth heat of her cheeks, which always seemed to be flushed. She loved his jokes (or at least she said she did, and amazed him by laughing at every single one). When she needed a hit of something, some kind of energy, she'd walk straight up to him and take one of his hands in both of hers and lay it on her chest, holding it square on the sternum, as if she could breathe him in through flesh and bone. Even when they annoyed the shit out of each other, when she yelled at him for playing the same song a dozen times at full volume, when he slammed around the house because she wouldn't get off the goddamn phone with her friends, they were together. Forever.

And then she died.

She'd felt crappy, but it was November, she thought it was some kind of persistent bug. She put off going to the doctor till Dan stood behind her at the bathroom sink one morning. In the cold white light reflecting off the tiles, he couldn't ignore the deep, dark circles surrounding her eyes. He'd marched her into the bedroom, stood over her while she called to set the appointment. And then it was cancer, it was her liver, there was chemo and radiation and it all went so fast, sometimes he thought they could wake up and it would be over, a bad dream.

But they never woke up. There was the hospital and the cemetery and the blur of tears and so goddamn much food. He had to throw it all out when people left, he couldn't choke down all those well-meant casseroles and cheerful, cloying cakes.

He'd stayed stoned out of his mind all the way through February. When the city began to thaw out, he'd started his pilgrimage. No destination, just walking the New York streets. He always moved fast, as if he'd had someplace to go. He always had his earphones plugged in, his feet keeping time to one old heartbreak song after another: Esther Phillips, "Please Send Me Someone to Love;" Otis Redding, "These Arms of Mine;" "I've Been Loving You Too Long to Stop Now"—the Cat Power version. Then Bettye LaVette's long, live version of "Let Me Down Easy"; Lorraine Ellison's single hit, "Stay With Me," like trying to stay upright in a hurricane. Jeff Buckley, "Lover, You Should Have Come Over," that one killed him every time, and he pressed replay, desperate to be annihilated anew. Dan wore shades until the sun went down, hiding red eyes from strangers. He walked until his feet bled, and then he walked some more, a soldier on forced march.

In April, tulips started blooming in their crowded little beds on the Upper West Side. There was a late snowstorm, and suddenly, snow on the bright pink petals and thick green leaves, too beautiful and too sad. He began to notice other walkers. They smiled at the tulips, and sometimes they smiled at him. He wondered how many of them were pretending to go someplace too. He made a new playlist, a lot of old music again, but this time the songs that Nikki had loved: "Witness" by Sarah McLachlan, tons of old Van Morrison—"Astral Weeks," "Beside You"—"Misty Roses," fucking Tim Hardin, she ate that up, the sixties stuff. How could she be so nostalgic for music she was too young to remember? He never got that. "Coming Back to You," Jefferson Airplane. He always saw himself at a window when it played; he saw her walking toward him, and his heart broke all over again, but he kept listening. Old Rolling Stones, the slow ones, "Angie," "Winter," "Fool to Cry." When he was alone at night, sleep was rare. On night in April, he unearthed his old guitar—it had been jammed behind a pile of boxes in the hall closet—tuned into his iPod and played along. After that, he played almost every night.

Spring came for real. The girls shed their heavy coats. When Dan got his coffee, he began ordering it to go. He took it to Washington Square or Madison Square Park to sit for a minute as he sipped. One day, an old man slouching on the other end of the bench made a sound, surprising him.

"Feh!" the man said, waving one large-knuckled hand at a stream of passers-by. The man was dressed in a dark-blue jacket and a striped tie, a pale yellow shirt, all clean and pressed, but worn soft by time. There was a brown paper bag beside him on the bench, the right size and shape to hold a sandwich.

Dan took out one earbud, just to be polite. He raised his eyebrows.

"Feh!" the man repeated. "Nobody talks anymore, always with the wires in the ears. Are they lamps or people? What happened to making conversation?"

"I still make conversation," Dan said, fibbing. He used to, of course, a million years—six months—ago. But not any more.

"How can you do that with these things in your ears?" the man asked. "This is the end," he said. "Everyone in their own private little world. Life ends this way, no one gives a crap."

Dan felt himself bristle. "I don't think you're right," he told the man. "I give a crap." That sounded almost true, surprising him. "It's so great to walk this city listening to music you love. What's so wonderful about listening to traffic, overhearing conversations, horns, squealing brakes?"

"And what's so great about listening to music?" the man asked. He looked simultaneously interested and skeptical.

Dan looked at the broken veins that made the man's nose resemble a road-map, the tufts of white hair sprouting from his ears. He thought about the possibility of a long life, realizing that until this moment, without actually knowing it, he'd been walking off the rest of his years, like this man was sitting out the rest of his. Dan realized that he wanted to live. He watched the walkers for a few moments before he responded. It was true, just about everyone who passed was wired for sound. "Think about music you love," he told the man. "What's your favorite?"

"Coltrane," said the man, surprising Dan. "A Love Supreme."

"Okay," said Dan. "Think about how you feel when you're listening to Coltrane. What if you could feel like that anytime you wanted? What if you have half an hour for lunch and you have to squeeze in an errand, but you can feel like that while you're doing it?"

The man was quiet. "You make it sound like some kind of medicine," he said eventually.

Dan felt something ripple through him, a shiver of recognition. "Yeah," he said, "I guess you could say they are self-medicating. But no health risks."

The man shrugged, tilting his head, giving Dan his due.

That spring, Dan told me, he realized that the only things he could stand to do were listen to music, make music, see movies, and visit museums. And after that day in the park, he had a name for this regimen. He was pretty sure he would've walked in front of a truck or jumped out of a window if he hadn't been able to self-medicate this way. But the big thing he realized is that he wasn't the only one. Everywhere he looked, everyone was doing it. He had a hunch that they mostly didn't comprehend what it meant, just like he'd missed its significance at first.

"It was like the world had been turned inside out," he said. "In the ordinary world before Nikki was gone, I'd read the *Times* every morning and pay attention to whatever the headlines told me was important. I had my job that everyone thought was so hip and cool, the only philosophy professor in a law school. I'd go on the road for a week or so—some conference or symposium, usually—and I'd be too busy to keep up with the news. When I came home, I'd pick it up where I left off. I hadn't really missed anything. After Nikki, the stuff I was supposed to care about seemed like one of those backdrops in a Road Runner cartoon."

I must have looked puzzled. "Does that ring a bell, Rebecca? Did you ever see one of those?"

I told Dan that was before my time.

"There'd be a long chase scene, and they'd loop through the same landscape over and over again behind it. You'd notice a mountain, a cactus, a shack, and then they'd come around again. I realized that was the news most of the time, just a repeating loop. People got addicted to it: that regular hit of fear, even though it felt bad, they had to have it.

"But after that conversation on the park bench," Dan continued, "the whole script flipped. When I paid attention to what people really cared about—I mean, like what did they do when no one else was telling them what to do? What did they spend their time on when it was purely voluntary? I saw that they were trying to connect—you know, moments of feeling, beauty, intensity—and how they did that was through art: music most of all, but films, visual art, writing, dance, the whole nine yards. *Art*."

I pulled out my iPod and recited the names of some of my playlists: "'Love songs,' 'Uplift,' 'Energy,' 'Nostalgia.' But to that man on the park bench," I said, "who was part of the other mind-set, none of that could mean anything, right? Just distraction or something like that."

"Maybe," said Dan, with a crooked smile. "Although I've always wished I had *A Love Supreme* on my iPod that day. I could have plugged him in and given him a taste of his favorite medicine. But, yeah, that was what kept the old paradigm anchored. People had been told what was important: wars, Wall Street, elections, moving product. The ones that believed it couldn't wrap their minds around the fact that while all of that was consuming busloads of money and energy, many more people were living in a world of sounds, stories, and images that made much more sense to them, that felt better, that meant more. That taught them something and aligned them with something that mattered, that sustained them during whatever insanity was going on day-to-day.

"If you pointed that out to the guardians of the old paradigm, they'd laugh at you. They couldn't conceive of any real alternative to worshipping whatever was grabbing the headlines. The truth just couldn't get past their assumptions. Music, for instance, was permanently embedded in the category 'entertainment,' so it could never ultimately matter. Something was happening all around them, but they literally couldn't perceive it."

"How did you operationalize that insight? How did you get from that to however many Doctor Feelgood stores there are now," I asked him, "and to all the other changes beyond that?"

"Over four hundred stores," said Dan. He shook his head a little, as if he couldn't quite believe it. "Sometimes I still fantasize about that guy on the park bench. What if I'd had the presence of mind to play him the music, and then what if I'd been able to turn to him and say, "In a decade, there will be hundreds of stores based on this principle? Anyone can go to one of them and get a kind of prescription for exactly what they need: playlists, movies, images, scents, tastes. It can be a one-time hit, or you can develop a relationship with a guide who really gets to know you, almost like a teacher or a spiritual counselor or a therapist. Man," Dan said, shaking his head again, "I don't think I would have been able to even name the levels then, let alone explain them. Let alone describe the impact this has had. But I still wish I could try."

"Describe it to me," I asked. "Pretend I'm that man. Take me through it."

"Well, the first thing to remember is that when a big shift comes down, for a long time it feels like things aren't changing," Dan said. "The old-order propaganda machine keeps broadcasting its timeless permanence. And then one day you look up and it's a new world. Back in 2009, you were in high school, right?"

"A big suburban education factory that I hated," I admitted, "where everything was about standardized tests. I spent most evenings dreaming up new ways to fake a sore throat and skip school."

"Something was peaking in those years," Dan explained, "and your cohort got the worst of it. The default setting for society was that everything could be reduced to data. We spent a fortune predicting things that couldn't really be predicted, and failing, and doing it again— and failing again. And doing it again. So dumb, but at the time, this sort of behavior was normalized, it was just the way things were. From where I sit now, it seems insane. Even scientific studies were showing how bad we were at prediction, but the people who claimed to base their thinking on proof weren't the least bit interested in disproving their own beliefs. So the whole juggernaut just kept rolling along.

"That was the year I read a book that opened this up for me—just a few months before Nikki died, in fact—Philip Tetlock's *Expert Political Judgment: How Good Is It? How Can We Know?* Back in the 1980s, he began tracking expert predictions, things that could be measured, like whether the Soviet Union or apartheid would last. He proved that the more respected the expert, the less accurate the predictions. The main effect of being treated like the world's foremost expert was overconfidence in your own flawed predictions." Dan smiled, all rueful amusement.

"By then, we had invested a huge amount of resources in things that treated real life as if it were a game with predictable moves. Real life kept right on not cooperating: the financial meltdowns, the uprisings in the Middle East, the mega-storms, it was endless. But tons of people remained loyal to that view of things despite its being proven wrong. Just like I said before about giving music its true value, if you were committed to the delusion of predictability—and remember, a lot of the people who were loyal to that bit of orthodoxy were major suits whose word came straight from God—to them, what we were saying was so alien, they couldn't really take it in. It was like," Dan gazed at the ceiling, stroking his brown hair with one hand, searching for an analogy, "like primitive doctors who bled patients to discharge bad humors. You know? Confront them with the notion of germs and contagion, and they just couldn't take it in."

"Okay," I said, "but I don't really get the connection. How does this lead to Doctor Feelgood? How does it lead to the big cultural shift people are starting to recognize?"

"Bear with me." Dan scrubbed at his beard again, searching for the right words. "In the old system, everything possible had to be scientized. Like the only valid measurement for kids' education was standardized test scores—you got that in high school, didn't you?"

"Indeed," I said. My biggest challenge in school was staying awake, especially during the endless test drills.

"The average kid in what was supposed to be a decent school was spending hours in class every day on a computer—no discussion, no interaction, just reading and checking off multiple-choice questions as if that were what learning is all about. We were training them to behave like machines.

"And not just kids. You couldn't call someplace and speak with a person. You had to go through a maze of 'press one' and 'press two' before they even put you in the queue for a human being. Half the time you'd drop off before you reached your destination and you had to start again. You could get furious, or you could get demoralized and give up. But whatever your reason for calling in the first place, if you stuck with it, you were being indoctrinated to obey automated commands, to get used to choosing from a preset menu, to stop valuing your own time. We were training ourselves to *be* machines.

"When I came up with the idea for Just Dan's, I actually thought I could fold what I wanted to do into that system. I was sure we could create a very detailed online questionnaire with really complex back-end programming to match people with music or movies or whatever would deliver what they were seeking. Like the old dating sites, you know. But it didn't work."

Dan remembered sitting in front of the computer to test out the beta design for an intake questionnaire. Jack, Mr. Supertech, had worked it up to his specifications, that was clear. But Dan noticed himself getting really frustrated with the questions. Coming from a machine, they felt intrusive. He kept wanting to give up. Subjectively, it took forever, although on the clock, the elapsed time wasn't any longer than a typical in-person session at a Doctor Feelgood's today. But what feels like a normal conversation in real time seems like forever if you're typing on a keyboard. Even with voice input being the dominant mode (and thought input coming on strong), time slows down when your conversation-partner is a machine. In the end, no matter how much they tweaked it, the thing was clumsy, like the old Pandora when you listed some unique genius as your favorite—Bob Dylan, say—and the program spit out a bunch of crap music that made you say, "Wait! How is this even related?"

"I was trying to figure out what was missing," Dan explained. "I knew it wasn't working, because none of the beta-testers had an aha moment, like standing up from the computer and feeling just thrilled with their new playlist or whatever. But I didn't know why it wasn't working. I tied myself in a knot trying to figure it out. Just for a break, this friend of mine persuaded me to go along to a kind of concert by a spiritual teacher who used music and chant to align people somehow. I thought it was probably more New Age bullshit—I'd had enough of that by late 2010, when this was all starting to come into focus—but I needed a night off. Then the teacher took us through something that changed my mind."

Dan could close his eyes and see the scene, clear and bright. This woman was wearing layers of long skirts and shawls. She looked like a miniature teepee. She held a small drum. Her name was Doria. He'd sighed and prepared himself for an hour or two of absolutely nothing of interest. He started going through his mental menu for something else to focus on while it was all unfolding. And then she'd led them in a series of surprisingly beautiful chants, targeting each one to what she described as an energy blockage in a different field: the body, she'd said, the emotions, the mind, and the spirit.

"First," he explained, "she said, 'let's clear out all that resistance you're carrying in here, the part of your mind that's saying this is all a little too woo-woo, that we're in New York, not some ashram.' And then she sang a melody so pure I literally felt it strike at my heart. It was like some shell melted away, and I felt the music enter my body. I breathed in and breathed out and it was like I came in for a landing. I was just *there*. I found myself all in one place for the first time in a long time." He looked up. "A long, long time."

"She taught us four chants, and then she asked if anyone needed help with a block of any kind, and then I was raising my hand, which was the last thing I ever expected myself to do. I told her about my problem with our intake questionnaire. I was pretty vague—I didn't want to give away any trade secrets, you know. But I explained the gist, which was that I had something that would really help people, but first, I had to understand what they needed. The trouble was, they didn't want to sit with a long online questionnaire, answering a lot of questions on the computer as the way to get access to what I was offering."

"Are you two friends?" Doria had asked, pointing to Dan's buddy Tim seated on his left. Dan had nodded yes. "So how well do you know Tim?" she asked.

"Well enough," Dan had told her. He'd known Tim since college. Tim had been at the wedding, and the funeral, and everything in between.

"So I imagine you could speculate about Tim's response to things, right? Like why he came here tonight, or how he feels about it?"

"Yeah," said Dan. "I can't guarantee I'd always be right, but we know each other pretty well."

"Let's say Tim was a total stranger. How many questions would your online survey need to give you the amount of information you're drawing on to guess his responses? A hundred? A thousand? A million?"

Dan had shrugged. "It isn't just data. I mean, you could list all of Tim's favorite music, but if you hadn't seen the way he was holding his head, or the expression on his face, or whether his body was moving in time to a particular song, you'd be missing a lot."

"That's right," said Doria. "I doubt you could equip anyone who doesn't already know Tim with enough information about all those nuances and gestures to beat you at guessing how he would respond to something."

"Okay," said Dan, wondering where this was going.

"Now, you and I don't know each other at all, do we?" asked Doria, pausing for Dan to nod his assent. "But you're sitting here in the front row, and I've been watching you now and then. Let me say a few things about what I've been seeing, and you tell me if they're accurate, okay?"

Dan felt even more exposed, but he nodded. What the hell.

Doria laughed. "Don't worry," she said. "I don't have X-ray vision. But it wouldn't take a Superman to see that you were pretty skeptical about being here. I'm fairly sure Tim dragged you along, right? I'm fairly sure this isn't the kind of thing you usually do." She'd looked at Dan with tender amusement, like someone regarding a child. "You just stop me when I get it wrong, okay?" She continued after Dan's nod.

"You have the look of someone who's waking up after a long nap, so to speak. I'm guessing something really hard happened to you, and tagging along with Tim, that was part of coming back to life afterwards. So the sadness is still there, but it's not the only thing anymore. Based on the way you asked your question, I'd say the big new thing in your life is your project, the one that has you stumped about the computer questionnaire. And I'd say you have some frustration about that: you can see what's not working, but not how to fix it."

Doria took a breath. "You're interested in women," she said, "but at a distance. So maybe the sadness is a divorce or something like that, and you're a little wary about getting hurt again."

"My wife died," Dan had blurted, "and it's been a year and a half." Doria's face fell. "I'm sorry," she said. "I didn't mean to be glib."

"Don't worry," Dan reassured her. "You made your point. Being present in the flesh, observing someone even for an hour, that tells you a lot more about that person than the answers to most questions. Now I just have to figure out how to use that."

"I started out thinking it was a time thing, too long in front of a computer," Dan told me. "But that could have been solved as bandwidth and download speed increased right along with speed of data entry—voice, thought, whatever. It wasn't the *quantity* of information or the time it took. It was the *quality*. The texture. The artificial intelligence geeks were sure that could be solved too, but I didn't believe it. I realized that no matter how good the human-machine interface got—no matter how seamless and invisible, how device-free and intuitive—nothing could replace our ability to draw instantaneously on a vast database of lived experience, our cognitive abilities, our emotional intelligence and intuition, not to mention things like our sense of smell and touch. Our high-tech romance had gotten us confused about what technology could and couldn't do—and should and shouldn't do. I never saw Doria again, but I'll always be grateful for that lesson.

"It helped me understand other things, too. Like the mainstream trend was toward really intense specialization. That worked well online. You had your Amazons, but you had a lot more really granular places to buy specific types of merchandise. If you knew exactly what you wanted, you had choice and freedom and ease. But with Dr. Feelgood's, the consumer didn't come in with a shopping-list. That person had a feeling, a desire or a complaint, that could be answered in many ways. You had to take in the whole person to figure out what was right, and that could only be done by another whole person with a calm presence and intuitive ability. And from a business perspective, once someone connected for the first time with a Virtuoso, all this optionality opened up: there was almost infinite room to move into new experiences and new products.

"It also occurred to me then that we were mostly blind to a basic fact. People were trying to come as close as possible to replicating human interaction online, without understanding that despite more and more technologies enabling communication at a distance, there is something about face-to-face and even skin-to-skin that we crave, that can never be replaced or even improved upon. It was like the old idea that e-readers would totally replace books instead of supplement them. Things last for a reason. Accept it, build on it, drop the big hubris about it."

Dan sighed then. "Once I got it, it wasn't all that hard to implement," he told me. "Unemployment was through the roof. In a rotten economy, most businesses were cutting customer service, but I realized that our entire gig was customer service. It wasn't some expendable feature, it was the essence of what we were trying to do. We put an ad on Craigslist. It was something like, 'Can you read people? Are you interested in music, movies, the way things taste and feel? Do you want to be part of something so new, it doesn't yet have a name? Amazing people, great workplace, good hours.' We got nearly a thousand replies the first day."

CATCHING THE WAVE,
CONTINUED
2033

A little prelude to the next section: Ten years ago, I thought Doctor Feelgood's was the best doorway into this story, because most Zeitgeist.com readers could connect to it somehow—they'd almost certainly heard of it, and probably visited at least once. But when I read Lulu the first draft of my opening section, she busted my chops bigtime. She accused me of *boutiquifying* The Wave.

For Lulu and her friends, abuse was built into a market economy. Capitalism equaled exploitation, QED. To be fair, I don't think she believed for a second that a centralized, state-run economy would have been better. She'd been a DIY kid, dumpster-diving for food, clothes, furniture, taking part in the whole hacking, recycle, and reuse movement. I think she had a vague vision of collective decentralization: just ignore the large structures of economic and political power, and let your own thing take shape organically.

That movement had a lot of energy when we were young, and it had an impact, obviously—just look around. In retrospect, it also seems like a precursor to (or perhaps just an emergent expression of) The Wave, in that it was determinedly human-scale, story-based, and prodigiously creative. But all such movements tend to an element of purism. People feel that the larger social order is a source of contamination, they fear cooptation, any compromise seems potentially fatal, and that tends towards a fastidious kind of rigidity. I loved Lulu like a sister, but she fit the profile.

Still, I could see the appeal in that view. There's always something easy and attractive about an us-and-them world: keeping your enemies straight imposes a comforting order on the moral universe. But that wasn't my nature. Everywhere I looked, I saw gray areas. Markets seemed to be the easiest—I'd still venture to say the most natural—way to distribute goods and services. Even Lulu's dumpster-diving friends held swap meets, primitive markets. Whatever vegetables they weren't able to salvage from behind Whole Foods, they bought at local farmers' markets for actual coin of the realm. They even bought stuff online. Maybe there was someone living a cave somewhere who could exist independent of markets, but not the rest of us.

So I began to imagine how it would feel to accept that markets were here to stay—that commerce was a building-block of human society, like families. I decided to enlarge my view to encompass both Lulu's pro bono world and Dan Kahn's business world, to look at the whole landscape of The Wave as one big ecology. I judged Dan to be a good guy, and I thought that if he existed, there had to be other good people in business. This sounds primitive, I know. But my thinking was just taking shape then, and I needed to hack a path through Lulu's outrage to a truth I could trust.

My roommate's fury built over several days: she'd walk into the apartment at the end of her workday and pick up the argument as if she'd just paused for breath between sentences. I really wasn't very good at conflict. It gave me a stomach ache. At one point, I actually thought we might have to part ways, which—given the tensions with my parents—felt like another looming family estrangement. Lulu and I had been roommates since I landed in New York.

So this felt terrible at the time. But in retrospect, it was enormously instructive. Lulu was coming from a left-wing critique of capitalism— and God knows that capitalism in 2023 deserved it, although there had been so many abuses and so many failed market solutions to social problems by that time, the tide had already turned against Wall Street and the multinationals. The campaign-spending scandal of the 2016 election was the last gasp, to state the obvious.

(Just to nod again to The Wave, I can't resist pointing out that Michael Moore's film about Lobbygate was the angriest and funniest release of 2017. *Highest Bidder* did more than anything to end the control of private money over elections. Then, when candidates didn't— couldn't—ride the gravy train to DC any longer, public outrage finally forced them to adopt serious corporate oversight and financial reform. I wonder how that old man who Dan Kahn met on a park bench would have responded to the idea that a movie was the last straw that triggered a change in our economic system? *Feh*!?)

I have to admit it: I was so distressed at Lulu's response to my draft, I nearly changed the story. But my editor thought I'd made the right choice by starting with Doctor Feelgood's. I had to agree that it would grab readers, so I sucked up my courage and stuck with it. But the next section of "Chronicles" would have been more true-to-life if I'd turned up the heat on Lulu's critique by a hundred degrees, instead of turning it down to a slow burn.

CHRONICLES OF THE WAVE,
PART 2: PRO BONO PUBLICO
2023

I asked my roommate, Lulu Francis, to review "Doctor Feelgood's Origin Story." Readers, she hated it, condemning it as crassly, egregiously, excessively commercial. Then we had a cup of tea and she agreed to be my guide to The Wave as it has emerged in nonprofit sectors: public provision, not-for-profit organizations, charities, and social services, all the work that gets done *pro bono publico*.

I couldn't have asked for a more knowledgeable (or more pissed-off) guide. Lulu's world is all about the public good. She always seems to be bursting with energy, this sturdy young woman with dark unruly hair and large brown eyes vibrating with intensity. She works at New York's Bellevue Hospital. After seven years on the job, she's a senior member of the hospital's storyteller corps, charged with patient interaction. If someone you care about has been in the hospital the last few years, you know what I'm talking about. The work of Lulu and her colleagues is conditioned on the understanding that every illness is in some sense unique to the person, and that every person is his or her own best ally in healing. Members of the storyteller corps greet patients upon intake (conditions permitting, of course: bullet wounds seldom allow room for pre-treatment stories). They invest enough time and attention to get to know each person, helping patients mine their own stories for their own best medicine.

Lulu has two sides, nicely symbolized by her displeasure at the first part of this series and her instant generosity in offering to show me the light. If you meet Lulu at work, you experience a skilled listener who spends much more of her time hearing from others than stating her own views. But outside the hospital, Lulu Francis isn't shy about expressing her opinions. Her seemingly unlimited patience easily gives way to anger and excitement. When she is angry, she quivers with outrage. Her eyes darken. She seems to expand. She makes an impression.

"You've got to be kidding me!" she said. "Doctor Feelgood's is in no way an emblem of the new culture! You're calling this 'The Wave,' right? So his shit is more like something that washed up on the beach. Broken plastic. You made Dan Kahn sound like some sort of guru, but he's nothing more than an exploiter in hip clothing. He had a good insight, sure—self-medicating with music, blah, blah, blah—but so many other people had it too. What he did was slap a brand-name on it and take it to the bank. He didn't invent anything. Maybe he believes his own propaganda, Rebecca, but you don't have to."

Lulu's muscular social conscience translates into an equally strong disinclination to trust power in any constituted form, including Dan Kahn's economic power. "If you put Dr. Feelgood's forward as the model," she told me, "people will think of The Wave as some kind of consumer trend, which really trivializes it. What is it, then? Some new thing for trendy creatives, like eating meat from named *terroir*? Where does the rest of the planet come into the story? What about the places where Dr. Feelgood's hasn't opened yet?"

Good point. That's when I asked her to guide me to people who could tell the rest of the story. That may sound like an invitation to be dumped on, but as I said, Lulu's excoriating political temper coexists with a gentle manner. It scared me at first, but by then I was used to the sudden shifts. She knows how to pit herself against an enemy and how to devise a creative protest. She also knows how to put herself on the same side as a patient, inspiring confidence, how to coax people to share their life stories. With her questions as the warp and the patient's responses the weft, Lulu co-creates something like a life-tapestry. She has developed a keen ability to know which threads to follow in pursuit of healing.

She's always coming home with storylines that reveal something important hidden in a person's inheritance. For instance, a patient may have heard since childhood that a great-grandparent died of "dropsy" without ever comprehending the nature of that ailment. Lulu knows how to track illness through the murky precincts of the past. On their joint journey of discovery, she and that patient will recognize that edema (which used to be called dropsy) can be a sign of congestive heart failure, and that may provide a clue to the patient's own challenges. Another clue may be growing up with a particular diet, or living with the daily tension of an unresolved conflict with a close relative, or spending years in a house perched on the edge of a stream that once carried a chemical corporation's toxic effluent. Each story unfolds in its own time, with its own boundaries and its own treasures concealed inside. The process of telling is healing in itself, helping the patient to feel seen, grounded, and connected.

At the hospital, what Lulu feels is just as important as the hard information she acquires. Part of her training was learning to read herself, to correct for her own biases and make a fair assessment of all that she sees and hears. Is a patient angry? Scared? Resistant? All three? Lulu has to be able to separate her own fear from the patient's: is she projecting, introjecting, intuiting?

She is adept at holding questions open, giving herself time to discover answers. Can she contact the parts of the patient that want to heal? How can they be strengthened? How can the voice of frightened resignation be soothed? How can she assist colleagues? How can a doctor's instructions to a particular patient be framed so as to increase that person's compliance with a healing regimen? Mostly, her focus is on individual stories, one at a time. But Lulu and her colleagues must also pay attention to the larger story that could advance medical care: how can their collective learning be integrated, deepening knowledge of disease processes and effective responses?

By the time I saw her the morning after she'd volunteered to be my guide to the pro bono Wave, Lulu had already set up a half-dozen meetings with teachers, students, community activists, clergy. Some were deep background, some became the profiles in this series. The first interview started the previous night, though. Lulu had the subject on speed-dial: her boyfriend Jacob Oumarou, whom she'd met eight years earlier, when he'd first arrived from Burkina Faso on a grant to study at the New School.

Jacob called himself a "theater worker," as distinct from "actor," "director," or any conventional way of describing a life in performance. He was a skilled and experienced actor, to be sure. He had trained in theater at the University of Ougadougou, graduating with honors. But that night, as he sat on the couch sipping tea, he explained that the work he was most passionate about didn't take place onstage. Jacob is slender, graceful in his gestures, soft-spoken in ordinary conversation— so much so, that it's astounding to see him in performance for the first time: who is this vigorous, dynamic presence? In conversation, he is gentle. He has an endearing habit of dropping his chin, gazing at you with upraised eyes. He loves Lulu in the most sappy, encompassing way possible, with pet names and little kisses, whispers every time I leave the room. But for once, he was all business.

In Africa, Jacob explained, "I understood myself as part of a long-term project of cultural reclamation. My parents didn't study African history in school. They studied French history and it had no meaning for the Burkina that they were trying to build—it was the colonialists' history, the made-up place they called Haute Volta, Upper Volta. My parents' generation had to learn African history after school. They try to teach people 'What is Africa?' 'What are African customs?' and generally, they are just learning it for the first time. In my generation, we have made more progress, but this condition—underdevelopment—has many meanings. When I lived in Burkina, our situation is by no means the worst in Africa, but we don't have enough schools, enough medicine, enough freedom, enough honest politicians. And the Burkinabe don't have the belief that they can get these things, so I must also say that we don't have enough hope." With a small, sad smile, Jacob shook his head.

"After university, I belonged to a theater for development team, traveling to villages, sometimes traveling days into the countryside from Ougadougou. In some countries, government ministries sponsor this work, but in my country, mostly the money comes from European foundations, UNESCO, UNICEF, big NGOs. The government lets it happen, looks the other way rather than supports it. And then you hope they don't look in your direction, because these are people who seized power through the barrel of the gun, and they don't intend to give it up. In the very nature of theater for development, you are for democracy, you are anti-tyranny, you are trying to liberate people, you are trying to raise their awareness. You are talking about their rights, making them feel that their rights, their lives, matter. Which is exactly what the people in power don't want." Jacob laughed. "Which is why I am sitting in the apartment of Lulu and Rebecca in New York, and not in Burkina."

I asked him to describe the work.

"I will tell you about one play about the need for clean water and how to get it. This was a big question in Africa—it's better now, but still not all better. Who owns the land where the stream runs? Do they own the water too? When I was a boy, there were parts of the country where you had to pay to have a drink of clean water, and those without francs, they drank bad water and got sick. Without education, the people may not understand how to avoid contamination even when they have access to the water. So there is a political story and a personal story and a fear of speaking too freely. We start with a family—always in the local language as much as possible—and then show how they suffer from contaminated drinking water. They learn how to avoid it. We give the information in writing too. And after everyone eats, there's a workshop. Always, we start with a story circle: everyone becomes part of the group by sharing a story about water, something from their own experience. When all have told their stories, everyone can see how they are the same, that we all need to drink and water our gardens with clean water, that we all face the same obstacles. Then we use the same methods to act out solutions: how can the people of this village pool their knowledge and work together for everyone's health?"

Jacob looked at Lulu. "Lulu says you are writing about the new culture. She says you call it The Wave, yes?"

"Yes." Lulu had her headlamp eyes trained on me. I felt as if I were under surveillance. I tried to focus on Jacob.

"When I started this work, some people thought it was a waste of money. Is it not better to send health promotion officers into the countryside to tell people what to do? Or just give them instructions from Ougadougou? We used to laugh, because, sure, if that worked, it would be much more efficient, no? If pigs could fly over New York, as Lulu says, they could deliver the mail! The thing is, it doesn't work at all. Why should people listen to a stranger who believes he knows everything and they know nothing, who takes no time to listen to their stories, who cares nothing about the reality of their lives?

"Today, everyone understands that this is the way we learn. So this is what you call The Wave, *n'est ce-pas*? Those who think people should be machines can say it is inefficient. But this is silly, no? Do we want to do what works, or keep doing what doesn't work? Now we know that those are the choices." Jacob shrugged.

"Say that people dump waste in the river upstream," he said. "The play shows how everything is connected. What goes into the water upstream flows into your drinking water carrying disease. The workshop is just as important as the play because when people tell their own stories, they see how those connections actually work in their own lives. It becomes not just an idea. They have lived it."

"Are you saying The Wave started in Africa?" I asked Jacob. "People here tend to date the big shift from the mid-teens—they see the signs really gathering in 2015 or so. And our friend Lulu has been telling me that there's a risk of seeing it as something for westerners with money to burn and time to spend at Doctor Feelgood's. But what you're describing—this work you did in theater for development, that would have been a few years earlier, right?"

Jacob laughed again. "The Americans cannot help but think they invented everything, hm?" He fished in his book bag and pulled out a report with a colorful multilingual cover: "Universal Declaration on Cultural Diversity," it read, "A document for the World Summit on Sustainable Development, Johannesburg, 26 August – 4 September 2002."

"This document is very important to me. I wanted to show it to you. I was in *lycée* when this meeting happened...."

Jacob was sent as part of a youth delegation to the Summit, and that was an honor. Getting off the shuttle and standing outside the Sandton Convention Centre in Johannesburg with other students, he thought he would burst from excitement. The tall, curving glass façade impressed him, the flags of all nations, the crowd of people in all colors and shapes, all kinds of national costume. Inside, at the welcoming ceremony, South African President Thabo Mbeki stood at the podium, proud and comfortable addressing thousands.

A large world globe occupied the space behind the president, and in front of the globe stood rows of South African children wearing the logo of the summit, ready to sing. The dancers and musicians who followed— incroyable!—he had never seen such costumes or such dances. All around him thousands of delegates watched, open-mouthed. And the speakers, heads of state, heads of important organizations and companies! He became friendly with the rapporteur for his delegation, who explained that many of them had come from homes like his. They had risen through their own drive and passion to become important people, people who spoke while the world listened. The rapporteur also told him not to believe everything he heard, that there were thieves and double-dealers even among the high and mighty. "Les gens ne sont pas parfaits." Jacob knew this must be true, but these fine individuals? It was hard to believe.

In memory the days blurred together. He hadn't always been able to understand the speeches—even with the simultaneous translation whispering in his ear, speakers used many words he didn't know. He could barely remember them afterwards. The music, the atmosphere, the feeling, yes. But the words, not so much. He quickly learned to ask for the transcript, and late at night, when it was hard to sleep from the excitement of being at this world-shaking event, he would lie in his dormitory bed and read the papers he had collected, struggling to make out words that were new to him. Still, his heart beat hard every time the words even hinted at the new world he was coming to know, a world populated by people who dedicated their lives to making things better.

Jacob held the papers at eye level, showing me their importance. "I have saved this document ever since," he told me. "By the time officials recognize a new truth, it is already out in the world. But I was a child in 2002, I had no experience. This was my first time to read the new understanding that tangible development—such as dams, factories, houses, food, and water—is linked with what they call intangible development, *le développement immatériel*. This was when I saw that both are equally necessary, that they must be part of the same thing. Listen to this." He read slowly:

Intangible development may be defined as that set of capacities that allows groups, communities and nations to define their futures in a holistic and integrated manner, stressing such values as participation, transparency and accountability. Intangible development, defined in this manner, is the critical link between cultural diversity and sustainable development. Cultural diversity enriches the pool of visions which mediate the relationships between meaningful pasts and desirable futures. The strength of this mediation provides a bridge to sustainability, since the major obstacle to sustainability has been the divorce between visions of tangible and intangible development.

"That is the speech of bureaucrats," Jacob said, "but the meaning comes through: people's stories matter, they should be in charge of their own development, it should be practiced with respect. In the late nineties and after, enough of this cultural work—theater for development was important, but not the only thing, not at all—enough of this work had been done that the big international agencies, even the World Bank—all of them—began to see that the old idea of development was unsustainable. It destroyed communities, wrecked the environment, robbed people of their land, their livelihood, their reasons for living. The development machine was like a factory to make refugees. They were clumsy about putting the knowledge into practice, of course. They believed that they could create a model that could be replicated everywhere. They still didn't see the problem in trying to reduce the work to a formula. But the insight was true. And that is the insight of this thing you are writing about, no?"

"Yes."

Jacob's smile faded; he suddenly looked very serious. Lulu's chin was propped on his left shoulder, mouth clamped shut, eyes blazing. "From a post-colonial perspective," he said, "What you call The Wave started in the developing world generations ago—not in America 2015. When Léopold Senghor and Aimé Césaire put forward the idea of *Négritude*, they were saying that what was dynamic and essential to Africa was culture, and that could not—and should not—ever be erased in the interests of industrialization and profit. Some say they went too far, rejecting all technological progress as a colonial imposition. Maybe so. But think about it: all the ways that the third world resisted *modernité*, all that the first-world powers dismissed as backwardness or superstition, this can be understood as people insisting on the right to their stories, no? And that is a seed of The Wave which has sprouted everywhere."

Today, Jacob works with a group called Witness for Youth which makes theater with young people, mostly refugees, who have suffered traumatic abuse. They use much the same methods he described from his theater for development work in Burkina Faso. I asked to observe, but he explained that these young people have suffered greatly, and they must be the ones to control the degree to which they expose their stories to others' eyes. By the time a group of stories has become a piece of theater for public performance, months of preparation and development have been invested in transmuting individual tales into dramatic shapes that can safely be shared. "If we are careful," Jacob told me, "the sharing completes a healing process, for the children and the audience. But we must be very careful not to reopen the wound, and that is what happens if you push someone who's not ready."

Lulu confirmed my contact info for the next day's visit to the Chinatown school where Witness for Youth meets after school hours. Jacob said I would like the principal. And I did.

Lisa Yoon's office at P.S. 124, Yung Wing School, looks more like a playroom than the wholesome-meets-sterile principal's office at the elementary school I attended. There's a large desk piled with papers, to be sure. But instead of dominating the room, it's in the furthermost corner from the entrance, surrounded on three sides with child-sized tables and chairs, shelves of kids' book, and a brightly painted wooden chest filled with well-used stuffed animals. A huge panda sits atop the heap. You can't see the walls because they are entirely covered by a mosaic of children's drawings. There are grown-up bookshelves behind the desk. One shelf held photos of Lisa and her partner Danielle—a doctor, I had learned from press archives. The others held books. I scanned the titles as I waited for the principal to arrive: progressive education's greatest hits of the last century, starting with Paul Goodman's 1960 *Growing Up Absurd*. I was leafing through that tattered paperback as Lisa Yoon walked in.

"Ah, yes," said Principal Yoon, "I wish I'd met Goodman. I love his writing and his story really engages me, the two faces of the intellectual and the man. Many contradictions. One of my professors at San Francisco State used to tell us stories about the time Goodman was a resident scholar at the Experimental College there, chasing lecherously after the students while remaining completely committed to engaging them with challenging and scholarly questions. High- and low-minded simultaneously. My professor used to say this was before the discovery of professional ethics. But I think the permission Goodman gave himself says so much about the old model of the male intellectual." She stuck out a hand. "You must be Ms. Price."

"Rebecca, please."

"Lisa," she said, shaking warmly. "So how can I help you?"

I explained my assignment, to chronicle the gathering cultural changes of the last decade. I told her I had the idea they had aggregated into a new pattern which I was calling "The Wave."

"Interesting. Why 'The Wave'?" Lisa smiled expectantly, eyes friendly behind gold-rimmed glasses. Most people didn't wear them anymore—the microsurgical alternative was so affordable, quick, and painless. I guessed that Lisa's glasses were there to make a statement about her seriousness. Probably a wise choice, given her appearance. No suit, just a pink shirt and khakis. Black hair in a neat schoolgirl bob. From my research I knew she had to be at least forty, maybe a bit older, but just going on visuals, she could have been a decade younger, my same age.

I described the Hokusai wave that had materialized in my imagination. "I have this overwhelming image of energy gathering force and taking shape. No one masterminds a wave, ordering all the drops of water into line. Many independent forces operate simultaneously—wind, gravity, disturbances of all kinds—and somehow, the wave mounts. I think that's how it happened."

"The Wave." Lisa tried it on for size. "You could be onto something. So how can I help?"

"Everyone says that P.S. 124 stands out among the New York schools that led the movement to change education. Most insiders name your arrival in 2014 as the turning-point."

Lisa stared at me for a few seconds. I couldn't read her expression: miffed, amused, nonplussed? "Well," she said, "the truth is actually very much like your description of a wave. I do think innovations are often introduced by outsiders, and I did arrive here with the intention to make changes. But it's not as if I was the first person to understand that the dominant way of seeing education was leading us in the wrong direction. Turn back the clock a few decades: read Maxine Greene or Debbie Meier. By 2011 you had Diane Ravitch, who'd been in love with charter schools and standardized tests, entirely repudiating her former views. Those women were thought-leaders before I was even out of college. Idealistic teachers everywhere admired their work. But they didn't command the kind of attention they deserved until around 2012, when the first domino started to fall."

"The first domino?" I asked.

"At least that's how I see it. There was growing opposition to test-driven education and all the accompanying cuts in arts and electives. Many teachers and more and more parents were up in arms over it. They had the SOS March—Save Our Schools—in the summer of 2011. A lot of us flew to Washington just to stand on the Mall in 100-degree heat and represent our truth. The movie star Matt Damon made a speech—it turns out his mother was a professor of education—and it went viral on YouTube. Have you ever seen that clip?"

I shook my head. Lisa fiddled with the touchpad on her eyeglasses, and a screen on the wall came to life. A handsome young actor, his head shaven for a part, one hand on his chest, attributed his success to teachers whose

> [T]ime wasn't taken up with a bunch of test prep—this silly drill and kill nonsense that any serious person knows doesn't promote real learning. No, my teachers were free to approach me and every other kid in that classroom like an individual puzzle. They took so much care in figuring out who we were and how to best make the lessons resonate with each of us. They were empowered to unlock our potential. They were allowed to be teachers.

"Wow," I said. "That must have felt good." I was getting an inkling of affirmation now, my ideas resonating in each interview. But to stand together with thousands who'd thought they were alone, that would have been powerful.

"It did," said Lisa. "And we started to hear that message more and more from teachers and parents. But to me, the first domino was Jerry

Brown's 2012 State of The State Address, his first after being elected governor again. He wasn't exactly famous for courage and insight, you know: more sizzle than steak. But somehow that made it more powerful. If you'd been listening with 'civilian' ears, you might not have thought the speech meant all that much, just a few mild rebukes to an excess of top-down policy and pointless testing, and a few words about listening to teachers. But if you knew how to listen between the lines, it was very good news. Finally, a state—a huge state with an enormous public school population—might be putting the corporate 'reformers' who controlled federal education policy on notice that it wasn't going to blindly take orders anymore.

"A few days later, Diane Ravitch keynoted a huge meeting in Sacramento—I was teaching there then. It was part of a speaking tour paid for by teachers' associations all over California. The organizers thought hundreds might turn out, but thousands of teachers and parents came to the event. They ate up her words and the words of all the other teachers who stood at the podium to testify. It was a little like Occupy in relation to the economy in those days: suddenly, you knew that your views weren't marginal in the way that the powers-that-be had tried to dismiss them. Actually, you might be in the majority, but a lot of organized money had been drowning out your voices.

"I can't point to any huge policy change that happened right away, but the ambient mood was different. Instead of feeling hopeless all the time and whispering in private about how much we hated teaching to the tests, teachers started sharing alternative lesson plans more and more, plans where kids learned through poetry or movement. Those things were woven into history and science classes side-by-side with other forms of teaching, not segregated into art class once a week or something like that. Change started to feel possible."

"How long after that did you write your manifesto?" I asked.

"I started it in the fall of 2012," Lisa said. "I circulated it to a few colleagues first, then revised it through the winter. A really good education blogger published it online right after the school year started in 2013. And then it just took off."

I read a little from *A Teacher's Manifesto*, Lisa's call to arms:

The corporate takeover of our public school system can only be stopped by teachers. For far too long, we've remained silent, and silence equals consent. All around us, so-called experts who have never taught anyone anything of use debate questions that will determine our children's futures, while we remain afraid to speak out.

But our voices matter. We know from experience what each child needs to grow and prosper. We know how much precious class time is wasted on test prep and drill, which do nothing to advance true learning.

It's time for every teacher in this country to stand up and speak out. If you are shy about doing it for yourself, do it for your students. We have the respect of students and parents, who will be inspired when they hear our truth. Together, we can turn the tide. And if we really care as much as we say, we can't wait a second longer.

"Pretty strong stuff," I said.

"It could have been stronger," replied Lisa. "Looking back, I'm nauseated by the extent that corporate profits determined education policy. You could say it was even worse than all the money corporations were making off of human suffering in overcrowded prisons, where they were making prisoners pay inflated prices for soap, toilet paper, using the phone. What they were doing in education didn't just sacrifice people who broke the law and got caught, it sacrificed an entire generation—or at least the majority who didn't have the money to evade the public system. I think the manifesto could have been a lot stronger, but I was cautious. Rather than drop a bombshell, I tried to find a way to write about it that would influence people who didn't totally share my viewpoint."

"Did it scare off the people who hired you to head P.S. 124?"

Lisa chuckled, shaking her head. "No. Actually, I think it got me the job. I heard that the higher-ups wanted to break the mold, so they thought it was best to hire someone who'd already declared herself, someone who's shown she knew how to deal with controversy. You know, get the hubbub over with on the front end and then just get on with it. And that's what happened. There was a pro-forma tempest in a teapot when I was hired, with all the corporate so-called 'reformers' denouncing me. Just about everyone else came to my defense, and what can I say?" She gestured at the surroundings. "Eight years later, here I still am."

Lisa was aware that she was making it sound easier than it was. Actually, it had been hellish. She knew withstanding criticism would make the system stronger. But she also hated being hated. She chose it anyway, but it got to her. For a month after she'd arrived in New York, she couldn't fall asleep without a pill. Every time she'd closed her eyes, the latest vicious smear ran through her mind. She'd lie awake composing her defense, even though she knew she probably wouldn't deliver it, and if she did, it would never convince her opponents.

None of the attacks were overtly racist. It was more dog-whistle language, allusions to an alien model of education being imported to New York—as if California were another country, or really, she thought, as if her being of Chinese descent made everything she did foreign. And when the alien stuff didn't do the trick, there was another round of even more vicious stuff about putting a lesbian in charge of New York's children.

Lisa had been trained to obedience. Like most children of immigrants, she'd been brought up not to make waves. She'd been a diligent student, a high achiever. There was this snide label—"model minority"—often applied to Asians in California. She was conscious of fitting the profile, at least up to a point. But she learned how to use it too. If a polite, smiling, neatly dressed, high-achieving Asian student spoke out one day to denounce a retrograde idea or attitude, people listened, at least in part because you were confounding their expectations. Her friend Jason said it was "the talking dog effect." "Yeah," he'd said, "they look at you like a dog that learned to stand on its hind legs and talk. You can take that extra credit to the bank, you know."

But Lisa had taken it to the world of education policy instead. In California, she'd benefited from lucky timing. So many teachers and parents were fed up with test-driven education that her words were welcomed as the articulation of what they were already thinking. But in New York, she'd been an outsider. There weren't real grounds for objection to her hiring as Yung Wing principal: the school population was more than eighty percent Chinese, so in no sense was she alien in that context. What they feared was her stated intention to make the school a model shaped by the values in her manifesto. They were worried that it might work—how if it did, that would shake things up even more. So they wrote letters telling her to go home and take her foreign ideas and perversion with her.

For weeks after they'd arrived, she lay in bed at night imagining faces distorted with hate, trying not to wake Danielle with her tossing and turning. As a way to channel her energy, she started writing for herself again: poems, mostly, or just a journal entry. It kept her quiet and took her mind out of problem-solving mode. She hadn't done any writing that wasn't instrumental for years: just reports, proposals, announcements, the occasional journal article. So that was one good thing about the time of tribulation.

And then it was over. Teachers, parents, people in high places came to her defense. That was gratifying. The hubbub died down to what she thought of as a normal trickle of hostility. Sleep returned. The memory faded. But she didn't want to leave Rebecca with a false impression that it had all been easy; she'd have to provide a little more background.

There was a knock at the office door. Lisa's assistant ushered in a small girl wearing a red T-shirt printed with "Yung Wing School." You could see that her long black hair had been combed with care that morning, had been fastened neatly with barrettes and elastics. But now, long strands protruded everywhere like the mad aftermath of a playground tornado. She stuck out her hand. "This is Amy," said Lisa. "Amy, meet Ms. Price."

"Rebecca," I said, bending down to shake. Amy looked me right in the eye, not the least bit shy.

"I'm your ambassador," said Amy.

"Each class has one," Lisa explained. "They rotate, month-by-month. The ambassador's job is to greet and host visitors to the classroom. We're headed to Amy's second-grade class."

As we walked through the halls, Amy explained that I was not the only visitor to her class that day. When she and her classmates had arrived that morning, they'd discovered a giant egg at the back of the classroom. "The egg is yellow, and much bigger than the teacher," Amy said. "But our teacher said not to worry." "Where do you think that came from?" she'd asked the children.

Amy and her classmates had walked around the egg, looking for clues. "We touched it and smelled it," Amy reported solemnly. "But it had no smell."

One boy—James, whom Amy described as "a little naughty, sometimes"—had wanted to smash it to see what was inside. But the teacher suggested that they wait to see if the egg hatched. In a little while, the egg started rocking, which was really exciting. "Everybody started yelling!" As it rocked, the shell began to crack at the middle, right at the place where you bang an eggshell on a bowl to empty it for cooking. Gently, the teacher lifted the top half off and set it on the floor. Inside the egg, dressed head-to-foot in yellow, was…a person, they thought, but Amy wasn't sure. "It looks kind of like a girl," she told me, "but when we said, 'Are you a girl? Where are you from?' it just made sounds, not words." She leveled a serious gaze at Lisa, then at me. "So I don't really know. But I think she's nice. I thought she might get mad at us for opening up her shell, but she didn't."

Lisa opened the classroom door onto a scene that resembled a very energetic game of charades. A female figure in a yellow catsuit was rubbing her stomach with one hand and gesturing toward her mouth with the other. "Hungry!" cried a boy. "Are you hungry?" The creature looked confused. "Let's try some yogurt," said a man who must be the teacher. He handed the boy a carton of yogurt and a few small spoons. The boy handed the carton and one spoon to the creature.

The creature smelled the yogurt, minutely examined the spoon, shrugged and handed them back with a quizzical look. Amy ran forward, exclaiming, "She doesn't know what they are. Maybe food is different where she comes from." "Maybe they eat bugs," another girl yelled. A raft of suggestions followed: "Worms! Dirt! Poo!" The teacher put a finger to his lips, signaling silence. "What do you think, children?" he asked. "How can we find out?"

"I know!" cried a girl, jumping up to seize the yogurt and spoon. "We have to show her how." She dipped the spoon into the carton of yogurt, and slowly slid it into her own mouth. "Yum!" she exclaimed, handing the creature the yogurt and a clean spoon. Looking at the girl for confirmation, the creature put a dab of yogurt on her tongue. Then she just held it there, rather than retracting it into her mouth. "Swallow it!" a boy said, but the creature just shrugged, looking confused and handing the container back to the little girl. Looking confident, the little girl mimicked the creature, protruding her tongue and adding a dollop of yogurt. Catching the creature's eye, she slowly retracted her tongue, chewed with extreme precision and deliberation, then swallowed loudly, using her free hand to trace the food's path down her esophagus to her stomach. Then she smiled, rubbed her tummy, and once again said, "Yum!"

The creature drew her own tongue back into her mouth, copying the little girl's actions. "Y-u-uh-umm," she said, laboring over the word. Then she looked surprised, rubbing her yellow stomach. "Yum?" she asked, gesturing at the yogurt. The children handed it back and watched her eat. When the yogurt was gone, one of them handed the creature a cup of water. The creature stuck her spoon into the cup and drew a teaspoonful of water into her mouth, looking surprised. The children laughed, and two more stepped forward to demonstrate the art of drinking from a cup.

Right before the break, Lisa introduced me to the students and their teacher, Rene Santos, who took me to one corner to quietly explain what I was seeing. The alien creature was a teaching artist who often worked with the school, he said, and this was a theater game called "Teach Me." It was a powerful learning experience, he explained. "In the traditional educational frame, second-graders are empty vessels: they know nothing, we know everything. It's what Paulo Freire called 'banking education,' where we drop knowledge into their minds the way coins are deposited into a bank.

"But this experience teaches the children how much they have already learned by giving them the opportunity to teach someone who really *is* a blank slate. It shows them that the way we do things—the skills they have already mastered—are not instinctive, but a series of learned behaviors. They experience themselves as teachers, and feel the gratification of teaching well. As the day goes on, we are going to teach this visitor how to walk and dance, how to say a few simple phrases, and how to behave toward others: how to share, how to say 'please' and 'thank you."

Rene continued. "Next week, we're going to study world cultures, so the students will get to encounter some customs very different from their own. 'Teach Me' gives them a framework to understand these as legitimate cultural differences, rather than viewing everything either as doing it our way or doing it wrong. They learn deeply because, as the teachers, they are completely caught up in the exercise. They talk, pantomime, lead, experiment, devise demonstrations. It's the best preparation you can imagine."

As Lisa and I walked back to her office, the halls filled with children making their way to the lunchroom. "When I was in school," she told me, "these experiential modalities that used creative, artistic skills would be sequestered into one or two classes a week. If I could bring someone from my elementary school through time to Yung Wing today, they wouldn't be able to tell me what class they were in: we use music and dance to study math, we make digital stories in science class and write poems about history. There are artists in every classroom, and every child has real opportunity to develop any strength he or she possesses. By the time I was in high school, teaching to the tests was the watchword, and most of our classroom hours were spent on rote tasks—quizzes, parroting back what we'd read in a book, drills. Everything was upside down. If someone was strongest as a kinetic learner, too bad. If someone had a great passion to interact with the world through visual images—the kid who filled the margins of his paper with drawings, for instance—that was a discipline problem, not a revelation of that child's essence and opportunity."

She sighed. "After things change for the better, the change can seem so natural and inevitable, you almost forget how hard you had to fight to budge the old order. When I hear that basic truth form in my mind—that there are many ways to learn, that every child is different, that every child deserves the opportunity to develop his or her unique capacities—I really have to struggle to remember what the counter-argument was."

"Money," I said. "At least from what I've read. Too expensive in relation to whatever they thought the per-person cost should be. Not quantifiable enough: the dominant idea of value relied on test scores and other numeric factors. A notion of education as merely preparation for certain types of workplace roles rather than cultivating the whole person."

"Yes," she said. "All that, of course."

She seemed a tiny bit annoyed. I bit my tongue. I'd learned that people didn't like someone my age delivering some definitive analysis of times they'd experienced firsthand. I got that: the official records never told the full story.

"Nowadays we call it 'factory education,' Lisa continued. "I have to remind myself that the people who espoused these viewpoints truly believed they were adopting reasonable positions. They told themselves they had a rational sense of priorities, that the alternatives were hopelessly idealistic. But I keep coming back to this gut sense of distortion, that they were blithely willing to sacrifice all of these beautiful little people to some utilitarian notion of practicality that wasn't even accurate. Even if you accepted their aims, it didn't get them close to the results they were claiming. I kept wanting them to admit that they were willing to spend infinitely more on war and punishment than on caring for children, and something was very, very wrong with that."

"And did they?" I asked.

Lisa shrugged. "A few did. When things began to change, some saw the light. But most kicked and screamed all the way to the end of the tunnel. What turned things around in the end was teachers standing up, joining with parents, and outnumbering everyone else. You can't judge success by whether or not you convert your opponents, but by how many allies you have. Simple, hm? But it took us a long, long time to get there."

"Stand up how?" I asked. "More rallies?"

"Sure, there were all kinds of meetings and rallies. But two national projects had more influence than anything else, and both used art—which makes sense, when you think in terms of means and ends being one. First, there was a theater company that—like many of them—based its work on oral histories, first-person testimonies from people involved with or affected by the issues central to whatever play they were making. You know Jacob's group? Like that, but this one wasn't around trauma, more around social issues.

"They'd done a production in their home state: a one-act play based on voices collected from teachers, administrators, parents, and policymakers. It looked at the way children were sacrificed to the bottom line. They toured it throughout the state—dozens of venues, libraries, schools, community centers, churches. They'd perform the script and then the second act, so to speak, was the conversation it sparked. There were always activists involved, so parents were offered clear ways to channel the energy the play evoked. It made a big difference to education policy in that state.

"So someone had the bright idea of making it national. They built a great website with all kinds of useful information. You could download the script and instructions for how to do a staged reading and a second-act conversation, and suddenly, there were a dozen readings every week in a dozen different places.

"The second-act testimonies were so great—so intense, diverse, touching—that someone got the idea of capturing them for digital stories. You know what I mean, right?"

"Who doesn't?" I shrugged. "I did a bunch of them in college, little three-minute movies with old photos, first-person narratives, found music. In certain classes, we could do them instead of minor papers. I really enjoyed that."

"Okay," said Lisa. "You can still see the archives online, but there was a huge blitz of them—all the people who spoke after these performances were invited to share their stories, and wherever there was a media center or some kind of media outpost, people volunteered to help craft and execute the stories. They say you're not supposed to launch a campaign around the holidays, but we decided to launch on Thanksgiving 2013—"If you can read, thank a teacher," you know, like that.

"By Christmas vacation, there were so many of them in circulation, you'd be getting stories by email every day of the week. The effect was to create the impression that every single parent and teacher was rising to speak their truth. The more first-person stories in circulation, the more mealy-mouthed the official demurrals sounded. And the thing was, the cost was completely decentralized. If you could get donated space, the cost of doing a staged reading was negligible. People donated time to teach digital storytelling, but in terms of out-of-pocket, again, next to nothing. It would have cost the centralized counter-campaign funded by corporations millions to get comparable saturation. They did spend millions, in fact, but no one noticed. They spent all their money on slick commercials blasting the same few images and slogans over and over again. But the tide had turned."

Amy ran past the door, evidently on a mission of some urgency. "Good-bye, Rebecca," she called. "Come back soon."

CATCHING THE WAVE,
CONTINUED
2033

One thing I learned from my research ten years ago is this: you can't really draw a map of The Wave. When did it start? Where did it spread? Each question leads to more. How can there ever be a definitive answer about something that was the aggregate of a million individual actions? Lulu saw the landscape through her own lens as an activist: she urged me to put the big social movements of the teens—Arab Spring, Occupy, clean energy—at the center of my narrative, as prime movers. But I was dubious about that. I reasoned that activism was not a new phenomenon. It had ebbed and flowed through history. So many aspects of those movements seemed the same as their predecessors.

I talked to older activists who pointed even further into the past: the twentieth-century women's and civil rights movements, because they taught us that everyone has a story and every story counts more than the old order recognized. That seemed true too: a sort of continuous opening out: an ocean, so to speak, and not a single wave. But I just wasn't sure these movements were part of The Wave *per se*. Maybe just fellow time-travelers.

But now, twenty years after Arab Spring began, it seems clear that Lulu was right. Those mass movements were fueled by individual stories in a new way. Their meta-message was this: *You think you can keep me down, but I am standing to be counted.* Although it was expressed in many different slogans, in the most varied places and on wildly different occasions, the unchanging through-line was a human story, a human face, against the faceless state or corporation. Not many names have stuck in memory: if you say "Mohammed Bouazizi" to someone in my generation, an image might surface of the desperate Tunisian fruit-seller who immolated himself at the beginning of 2011 and started a revolution. But mostly, we remember the no-leaders character of those movements: we see a sea of disparate faces, young and old, every color, condition, gender. These vast assemblies of individuals resist cohering into a mass, let alone a single face.

All of us remember "mic check" from Occupy. In the original encampment in Zuccotti Park near Wall Street, the police forbade protesters to use amplified sound. So they developed a special way of communicating: a speaker would call out a phrase, and successive waves of protesters would repeat the words until they had been heard in the farthest rows. This had the effect of slowing everything down, a good antidote to the precipitous action that might otherwise have taken hold of these crowds. But it also had the effect of highlighting the value of each individual, of expressing a shared eagerness to safeguard each other's equality as participants in a deeply democratic movement. I could see how that desire was rooted in earlier liberation movements that were still rippling across history. It wasn't that we'd attained absolute racial and gender equality, or that some people didn't hate women or gays or Latinos just as much as in the old days, but there was evident progress, hard-won and ongoing.

I was a student at the time. I hadn't met Lulu yet, but she was in school too, in the thick of Occupy and much else, while I watched from the sidelines. I could sense the excitement and possibility of being part of a movement. But I could also see the negative aspects highlighted by the press at that time: how, within a framework of decisions built on consensus painstakingly communicated by hand-gestures, one person with crossed arms and determination could stop anything from happening. One person with a black mask could turn a democratic assembly into a nasty spree.

Now I see that my perception was skewed by encountering these movements largely through the mass media. I couldn't perceive the emergence of The Wave in them, because the writers and broadcasters who were framing the story for me couldn't yet bring The Wave fully into focus. They were trying to understand everything through the lens of the old paradigm which was biased toward dismissal of any emergent phenomenon, toward anything that might contradict the presumption of an order in which the same people would always be calling the shots.

But by 2020, with the success of the Victory Garden campaign, things fell into a new shape. Up through most of the teens, two futures had contended in popular imagination. Although there were brave evocations of our collective creativity and capability, mostly on the liberal-to-left side of the aisle we saw the end of the world approaching. Think of the we-can-do-it segment tacked onto Al Gore's 2006 film *An Inconvenient Truth*: after watching those animations of the coastlines receding, my 14 year-old friends and I sincerely doubted that recycling would save the planet. Throughout the ensuing decade, the dystopian view became more dire and more insistent.

Meanwhile, the right wing harked back to Ronald Reagan's "morning in America," continuously broadcasting a simple counter-narrative: *We are smart, ingenious, and strong. God could never destroy the best country on earth with made-up terrors like "global warming." American virtues will save us and send the scaredy-cats running.*

Toggling back and forth between these two views always ended the same way: in a fatigue bordering on exhaustion, followed by an intense desire to lie down and watch TV.

Getting private money out of politics was the prerequisite to attracting strong, responsive candidates who weren't owned by corporations and didn't spend most of their time begging and trading favors for money. Across the country, people organized with great energy and determination around this issue, which set the scene for change. But it was slow. Really slow. Finally, what pushed it over were the egregious excesses of the 2016 campaign, which showed voters something they just couldn't swallow.

I don't know if I can do justice to the impact of the Public Election Financing Act of 2017—for so many of us, it was some kind of miracle. We had lost faith in the notion that laws and public policies could have positive effects. Then suddenly, stunningly, a shamed Congress—with more than a dozen seats up for special elections because their original occupants were being prosecuted for corruption—passed a law that transformed federal election campaigns from a bazaar of influence (largely indifferent to the public interest) into something like actual democracy. Once PEFA passed in Washington, the states followed suit. It became impossible to resist a tidal wave of public outrage; it surged across the landscape, scrubbing away the stink of corruption.

A year later, the smartest, best-coordinated environmental action campaign this country had ever seen made "Victory Garden" the most viral meme in history. But before I tell that story, I have to set the scene, because in a very odd way, new developments in psychological research were the key to it all.

There's a pretty clear consensus today that the most important scientific advancements of these years had to do with understanding our own minds. Some of that work focused on our brains: neuroplasticity, for instance: we could alter neural pathways through meditation, scientists discovered, and brain functions could be relocated to route around injuries. Equally important was psychological research that demonstrated how our minds actually work, creating an alternative model to the old notion of decision-making as a matter of rational actors performing calculations. In 2011, Daniel Kahneman's big book

Thinking, Fast and Slow summed up a lot of this work in ways that non-specialists could understand. It stayed a best-seller for months, popularizing the notion of a mind housing two very different thinking systems. You could quibble with minor points in Kahneman's work, but overall, his case was devastating to our old ideas about human thought.

Nowadays, we all talk in terms of System 1 and System 2 without even thinking about it. We know that even when really important things are at stake, our mental "operating system" tends to default to System 1, making quick, intuitive judgments strongly influenced by images, associations, and emotions. We know that something has to disrupt System 1's smooth workings for System 2 to kick in. Slow, conscious mental processing happens when we actively choose it, or when complexity or difficulty require that we take pains to understand something. When I first studied psychology in college, we understood that people were making decisions based on hunches and feelings where careful consideration could have been better. But we saw it as some kind of individual failing: people were lazy or stupid or didn't care enough to invest the effort in rationality. By the time I was a senior, the framework had already begun to shift to understanding what is, to finding a way to work with it without making it into a moral judgment.

Today, we know that this dual system is just the way our minds work, neither good nor bad, merely *what is*. With the acceptance of this new model, people began seeking to affect public opinion in much more sophisticated ways. It wasn't universal. Political persuasion had kind of a split personality then. The right had no qualms about addressing System 1 through the use of clever frames, symbols, and associations. But often, progressives saw that as some type of moral failing. Instead of targeting System 1, they kept chiding voters for their refusal to embrace the wonkish wisdom of policy papers. Beginning around the turn of the century, a new profession came into being that bridged the gap. Cognitive scientists and linguists hung out shingles as "framers," specialists in figuring out how to frame ideas for maximum receptivity based on what was being learned about cognition. By the time of the "Victory Garden" campaign, they'd finally figured it out.

The first step was annexing something like ancestral memory. During each of the twentieth century's world wars, governments had promoted home vegetable gardens as a way to offset food shortages and invest people in the war effort. They'd caught on in a big way, giving women, children, and elders—relegated to the home front while men went off to war—something concrete to do, something that felt worthy and significant. Plus there was pleasure in the gardening and the eating that added to the experience. The original victory gardens accomplished two goals: the practical goal of adding to the food supply, and the equally important goal of aligning people's spirits with the war effort.

Many decades later, leaders of green jobs groups, environmental organizations, and their allies faced a comparable problem: without a mass mobilization that could force government and industry into major policy changes, a terrifying future would unfold. Oil was peaking, and big energy companies were blocking almost every attempt to replace carbon fuels, even as they accelerated practices like fracking where no one knew the long-term consequences. Drastic weather events triggered by climate change foretold more disasters like the devastating tsunami that hit Japan in 2011. Major changes were needed in the way people lived, reducing our energy consumption by staying local, driving less, replacing toxic technologies with clean ones. But corporate profits skyrocketed with scarcity, so many corporations—not just Big Oil—resisted investing in change. Some analysts said their reluctance was based on economic uncertainty, but another diagnosis seemed more accurate: reporting record profits to shareholders was a much higher priority than good corporate citizenship.

The other side's slogan was "People Not Profit."

For ordinary citizens, day to day, life's texture still seemed fairly normal. There was no sign California was about to slip into the sea. The sun rose and set on time. In a way, even the best-grounded warnings still felt like scare stories. Beyond that, even those who were convinced by the warnings found it hard to believe that their own actions made any difference. That seat-of-the-pants feeling—*Let's get moving! This is up to me!*—seldom kicked in for even the well-informed, and an alarmingly large portion of the population still got its information from sources insisting that climate change was a lie.

The Victory Garden campaign was conceived as a way to hitchhike on widespread and profound belief in Americans' neighborly tendency to pitch in during a crisis. The message was seldom spelled out in as many words, but the imagery, memories, and feelings it encapsulates informed the campaign. If you were privy to the strategy documents, though, you could read the ideas behind it all:

Who are we? What do we stand for? How do we want to be remembered?

Almost a hundred years ago, our economy crashed, leaving millions homeless, unemployed, and desperate. Across this country, we can still see what our grandparents and great-grandparents did to rebuild: parks, highways, dams, amphitheaters, post offices, all the great things possible when a nation pulls together as one.

That set the stage for our response to World War II, when Americans planted Victory Gardens, collected scrap metal, and sent care packages to loved ones fighting overseas.

Today, America is threatened by enemies far more frightening than foreign powers: Big Oil wants to squeeze us for every last drop; and multinational corporations don't care about poisoning our air and water, so long as record-breaking profits roll in.

Once again, we are calling on every man, woman, and child to pitch in. This whole country is our Victory Garden, and the incredible strength, goodwill, and commitment of the American people are needed to make it flourish. If we don't act now, we stand to lose everything. If we do act now, future generations will thank us for the legacy of love and wisdom we left for them to enjoy.

All the major environmental groups signed on. Working together, they reached many millions. They all linked people to a single mega-portal and app with a powerful signup system, where anyone could access personal action-items, volunteer tasks, community projects, and activist opportunities. The core idea was to get people personally active in real time, not just at their computers. As soon as you signed up, your information was channeled to a local group, and an actual human being called with an offer to give you a ride to a meeting or an action, or to walk through your house to help evaluate your energy usage and find affordable alternatives where needed. You got an invitation to a picnic at the community garden, or an offer of help in digging the soil for your own vegetable garden. Rooting people in relationship was the key: the first step was connecting every single person with neighbors in a positive way, and because that felt good, the next steps were easier.

But the genius of the campaign was how it got people involved in the first place. A remarkable cadre of organizers, spiritual leaders, visual artists, musicians, actors, and filmmakers agreed to contribute their names and their time. On the day the campaign launched—Earth Day 2018—a new clip was released every hour on the hour. They weren't very talky, because all of them integrated the imagery behind the message: barn-raisings, Victory Garden clips from World War II, footage of V-E Day in Times Square, JFK's "Ask not..." speech. They posed the three questions, offered some variation on the theme that "Your country, your community, your neighbors, and future generations need you now," and left the clear message that the difference between defeat and victory was in your hands. They all clicked through to the cloud-based portal—via the app, if you were viewing on a mobile device or augmented reality headset—which could handle an unlimited number of interactions.

Some of these digital stories featured favorite musicians performing songs written for the occasion, or actors in scenes evoking embedded memories of the historic power of mutual and self-help. Others featured beloved personalities telling first-person stories of their own families' survival in prior crises and invoking our care for future generations. The clips flowed steadily every day, hour upon hour. They all had an interactive feature that enabled direct participation: after Adele or K'naan or some other major statesperson of popular culture told his or her tale, there'd be a prompt: "What about you? Tell the world."

You could instantly upload your own photos or video, narrate or write your own script, or you could improvise, just speaking whatever came to mind. People were thrilled with the first augmented reality glasses then, so there were quite a few clips that were basically narrated walks through places that needed saving, journeys through the maker's eyes. Or you could tell a story about your own ancestors, or describe what you were personally planning to do to move the campaign along. You could ask for neighbors to help you make a garden, or organize a carpool or a buying co-op for green cleaning products—whatever you needed, with a feature something like the old Kickstarter, but about recruiting volunteers rather than raising funds. Because of the readymade framework, every clip went out under the Victory Garden brand, and every one linked recipients directly to action. You could send whatever you'd created to individuals as well as to the portal, so there were quite a few conversations that ended up using the Victory Garden as their medium of communication.

People tried to mess with it, of course, but the frame was really robust and very hard to break, so anyone who tried to pour anti-Victory Garden content into it would have to accept that recipients were going to experience the pro content first. The counter-message never seriously disrupted the flow.

This kind of crowd-sourced campaign is commonplace now, of course. But at the time, it took the country by storm. Not since Occupy had there been such strong emphasis on individual actions, such a strong incentive to take steps. And everyone who acted on the invitation, sending out a clip, reinforced the invitation to their friends and family members to do likewise. I don't know that there's ever been a definitive count on how many digital stories were generated in the Victory Garden campaign, but certainly millions. In the first month alone, the portal registered more than sixteen million visitors, roughly equal to the number of downloads of the app, and millions more accessed the material in other ways. The campaign transformed this country's relationship to the environmental crisis with a raft of new regulatory initiatives, the President's declaration of "War on Climate Change," and a enormous, decentralized new infrastructure of community gardens, energy co-ops, public transit plans, electric car and bicycle banks, tax credits for energy-use reduction. A definitive shift toward locally based development drastically reduced the need for fossil fuel consumption. And above all, serious regulation of corporate practices, plus enforcement with real teeth.

Looking back, I'd have to say that the relative stability of our coastline today—not to mention the general level of neighborliness and optimism—is down to The Wave.

CHRONICLES OF THE WAVE
PART 3: THE BUSINESS OF AMERICA
2023

Guillermo Ford did not fit my mental image of a corporate CEO. That person was white, hearty, and grey-headed, whereas Guillermo Ford ("Will," he said, extending his hand) was the color of Vietnamese iced tea, the kind they make with condensed milk. I knew from his corporate bio that he was 42, young to have climbed so high on the corporate ladder. He had friendly eyes, round, handsome features, and a gentle manner that immediately put me at ease.

Smiling, he said, "Okay, let's get it out of the way."

"Get what out of the way?"

"How I'm not what you expected."

"Busted!" I laughed. "So do you get that all the time?"

"From people who aren't in business, sure. I don't know with absolute certainty that they expect me to be fat, bald, white, smoking a big cigar, with dollar signs for eyes. But I have a hunch I'm not far off the mark."

"You should meet my friend Lulu," I told him. "She'd say you forgot the roll of dimes John D. Rockefeller used to carry in his pocket to hand out to urchins."

"Seriously, though," said Will, "I worry about this, that selling goods and services is an essential part of any society, yet a sizeable contingent of this one finds the whole thing morally suspect. If you're in business, you must be an exploiter. C'mon," with a sad shake of the head, "exploiters are everywhere. No one's immune: artists, priests, union organizers, even some of your fellow journalists. And as for non-cigar-smoking, relatively youthful CEOs of color, there are more and more of us every year. Condemn exploitation, sure, but don't throw the baby, the bathwater, the tub, the towels out the window too."

The way he paused then to twinkle at me, waiting to see if I got both the joke and the point, took the slightest edge off my relaxation. I imagined him anticipating and addressing all my reservations, which suddenly made me feel very young. But I sucked it up and I told myself that was good for journalistic objectivity (just in case it existed). Then I nodded, proffering the expected half-smile.

"Of course," I said. "But I came to see you because your company has a reputation for innovation. What I told you about my story—the whole idea of what I'm calling "The Wave" and how it came to be— it's impossible to see what I'm even talking about if you omit the green businesses, socially responsible businesses, high-tech social innovators, and social entrepreneurs. For this story, I could not be visiting a manufacturer who was in trouble for toxic emissions."

"So we both understand." Clasping his hands, Will waited for my questions.

"My interest is in how things came to change, and what the impact has been," I said. "People always put you on the top ten lists of major business innovators of the last decade. Can you give me the story from your perspective? Fortunato is a design company, with its fingers in a lot of sectors: furniture, other home design, product packaging, corporate identity. You have offices in six countries, more than a thousand employees." I gestured at the elegant furnishings, the sky-high view. "How did you come to be here?"

Will punched a button on his phone and said, "*Café con leche, por favor,*" glancing at me. I nodded.

"There is a career path that sometimes brings people like me to the top: striving immigrant parents, bright kid, luck. I was born in Puerto Rico, but my family moved here when I was very small, so I went through school here in New York, from P.S. 96 all the way through business school—on a scholarship—at NYU. I found out that being smart, capable, and thoroughly bilingual put me in demand, because multinationals had divisions in every part of the world, and they needed people who could be nimble and fluent in two cultures, not just two languages.

"But what I think gave me the biggest advantage in starting out at Fortunato Latin America was minoring in art. I did it—over my father's objections—because I'd always loved to draw and paint. I didn't think I could make a go of it as a professional artist; the competition is crazy. But I reasoned that if I did well in all my business requirements, it wouldn't hurt me and I would enjoy college more. At least, that's what I thought for most of my time at NYU, till my graduate adviser looked up from my transcripts and said, "'The M.F.A. is the new M.B.A.,' hm?"

"Daniel Pink."

"Indeed. In 2004, he began using that line and it went viral. So I was lucky. My personal ambitions and desires naturally melded with something that was emerging at the time, and that made me look as if I were ahead of the pack. I can't actually take credit for that. Just lucky." His dark eyes disappeared into a wide smile.

"So I took what was a fantastic job for a recent graduate, midway up the ladder in the Latin American division of corporate. My father told me to keep quiet, pay attention, watch and learn, and I did that for a little while. But some of what I saw seemed crazy. A global enterprise based on good design—which requires both beauty and practicality, yes?—that had designed its corporate culture to be exactly like a bank or insurance company.

"We met at long tables in perfectly clean, quiet, colorless rooms. Everyone was dressed for success and on best behavior. We observed the pecking-order, deferring to those in authority, taking care not to propose anything that would put us too far ahead of the pack. The optimal intervention was to suggest something that added a single new detail to a product already deemed successful. You'd look around the room and most people were texting, surreptitiously doing other paperwork—anything but being there. I began to reconsider my choices. I was busy, and as far as I knew, the higher-ups thought I was doing well. But I was bored.

"One day, I was sitting in one of those meetings....

Will could see the scene in his mind as clearly as if he were right there. Everyone had been talking about packaging for a new fortified juice augmented with extra vitamins and minerals. Bottles filled with brightly colored liquids sat on the table, the only spots of color in a room of beiges and sands and off-whites. Will stared at the bottles, letting his focus soften until they were colorful blurs, like spilled paints. He began painting in his imagination, orange running into blue into an intense magenta. His vision began to pulse. Suddenly, a powerful image flashed through his mind, a Santeria drum ceremony he had witnessed as a child on a visit to Loíza, his father's village. He saw the Santera dressed head-to-toe in white with just a flash of blood-red, the drummers, the dancers, candles, fire, the dead bird with its smell of blood, the plates of food offerings, the blazing flowers. Everything pulsed in unison, beating like a heart.

That day in the conference room, it was just a flash, but very complete: sounds, colors, smells, all seen through a kid's eyes. Will had been ten years old on that trip. Mostly, it was fun—playing in the water, walking through the hills—or boring, relatives pinching his cheeks and feeding him until he thought he would burst. But the Santeria ceremony had scared him a little, the pulsing intensity of it all. It was imprinted like a photograph. Just now, returning there had been like flipping TV channels, a glimpse of an alternate reality coexisting with the meeting going on around him.

"If I'd been at dinner with friends," Will told me, "I would have mentioned it without hesitation: 'Wow! I just saw something so different from the here and now. Let me describe it to you. Hey guys, help me figure out why it flashed through my mind, what it means.' But there in the boardroom, you didn't talk like that. Especially *I* didn't talk like that, because even though my Puerto Rican heritage was an asset to the company, it was understood that you played it down. Your prime directive was to show you could fit in, talk the walk, execute the culture with leaders from elite backgrounds and with a company that—despite its multinational character—belonged to the white world. I looked around. Someone was presenting numbers on the target demographic for this juice, everyone else was trying to look interested.

"Instead of getting with the program, I started to wonder. What if everyone had permission to share the quick flashes of memory and inspiration that were running through their heads? What would that conversation look like? Would we spark new answers to the packaging challenge that way? What if someone started drumming? What if we got up and moved around the room? What if we made a call-and-response out of the product names? What if we took these flashes as guidance, not distraction? I started to wonder what everyone else was experiencing but not saying.

"Up till then I'd been thinking that all there was to my colleagues was public persona, everyone's office persona was who they truly were. But of course, there had to be just as much more to them as there was to me. It's just that none of us had been bringing all our capacity to the job. We parked half our selves—memories, dreams, passions—outside the door, and picked it up again when we headed home. There was all that capacity the company wasn't getting.

"That's as far as my insight went that day. It all occurred to me as a problem-statement: why does everyone in corporate offices leave so much of themselves home? How was I going to be happy spending the rest of my life in an environment like that? It didn't take that long for my mother to get tired of listening to me fill my weekly calls with complaints. '*El mundo es de los audaces*,' she said: 'The world belongs to the bold.' I thought yes, she's right, I'm young, if this isn't working for me, I can find another job. What have I got to lose by saying what I think?"

Your job, I thought but didn't say. "Uh-huh," I said. "So what happened?"

"I went to the division head and told him I wanted to pull in a few people who were at my level or below to create a design lab within Fortunato Latin America. I cited Daniel Pink, Steve Denning's storytelling books, the 2010 IBM CEO study about creativity—all the literature that was surfacing in those days about innovation and improvisation being key capabilities for the new business environment. I told him I was well-suited to do this because of my art school training, and that I'd met other people in the company who were musicians, actors, dancers. They already had the skills. I said it could be simple, elegant, and practically costless, because the innovation was to pull people into a team that supported creativity. We didn't need a new office. We didn't need major equipment that wasn't already accessible, just a space, a budget for supplies, and the freedom to deploy ourselves where we were needed. I knew that if this took off, we would have to bring in outsiders whose skills levels were far above our own, and that would cost money. But I figured that if we succeeded, that could easily be justified by the results.

"We'd make ourselves available to projects across the division that wanted creative energy. People could spend a day or two with the team focusing on their projects. If something good came of it, we'd be available for more. I asked him to give us six months to see how it went, and at the end, if he decided the experiment had failed, I would accept that."

"Did you feel you were innovating not just within the company, but within corporate culture?" I asked Will. "I've been reading up on something called 'arts-based business learning,' which has been around for a while."

"I didn't feel I'd invented sliced bread," he said, if that's what you're asking. In business school, we'd studied some of that literature too, and they gave us the opportunity to dip into many different creative planning modes. But by and large, that was seen as a sort of spice or *salsa*: there was the usual way business was done, and then sometimes you had a team of arty consultants in for a day or two to shake things up. Making it part of the division's ongoing work, redeploying people who were under-used in the old corporate culture, that was my value-added. I had a high degree of confidence that it would work. I saw very little chance that it would fold after the initial six months. I bet my future that it would work so well, leadership wouldn't want to go back, and that's what I said to everyone: if you don't believe enough to put skin in the game, deal yourself out.

"Instead of a small design lab within the organization, what I imagined was an organization that was almost all design lab, with smaller territories staked out for basic infrastructural tasks: financial management, supply chain, building maintenance." He shrugged.

I smiled. "I know a little about how this story evolves," I said. "And as far as the world is concerned, you got your wish. How long did it take?"

"Well, that first design lab was in 2012. The Latin American division posted such a huge uptick in 2013 when we integrated design-lab ways of working across the organization, I was asked to join global corporate in 2014. I was appointed CEO three years ago, in 2020. So that was eight years from the first beta-test, which is a good long time. But it seemed fast, like being swept along. I had a friend on that first team who was big on hockey metaphors: we tried to see where the puck was going and skate to the puck, he says. And it worked pretty well. A lot of action in those days. I never felt bored again, that's for sure."

"The Wave," I said.

Will pulled out some photos of a conference room at Fortunato Latin America. It had that airport-lounge look: could have been anywhere or nowhere. Lots of glass, pale curtains, pale carpet, pale walls, long, polished wood table, upholstered chairs on rollers, flip-chart, video screen, a sort of kitchen corner with a sink and refrigerator, coffee-making apparatus.

"These are the before shots," he said. "This was our basic team working environment before the design lab." He stood. "Let's take a walk. I'll show you how it looks now."

Think of the best-equipped playroom imaginable, for adults. We stepped into a large, flexible space. It was pretty open, but Will showed me how it could easily be divided into a series of smaller rooms. Along one wall, shelves and cupboards held a remarkable variety of tools and supplies: paper, paints, pens, to be sure; but also video equipment, musical instruments, bins of costumes and props, mats, easels, modular furnishings that could be stacked in different shapes and configurations. A bank of equipment for playing music and moving-image media, backed up by an extensive digital library. One long wall is all modular screens, so you can view still or moving images at any size. There's a 3-D printer, one of the new compact models. There's a well-stocked kitchen at one end, and up against one wide floor-to-ceiling window, a cleverly designed vertical garden of aromatics, rows of green herbs and other fragrant plants.

We walked past small groups of engrossed-looking people seated here and there at tables and on couches. Will introduced me to a bright-eyed young woman working alone in a corner. "Sandra is one of our staff artists-in-residence. They're all fantastic at facilitating creative processes." Sandra smiled.

"What's your specialty?" I asked her.

"My background is in theater," she said. "We use a lot of Playback, Forum, theater games—are you familiar with those? I can explain."

"Familiar enough," I said. "But maybe later I can observe you working." I looked at Will, who nodded.

"We still have the kind of long table that old-style businesses use for large gatherings," Sandra said, "but this one breaks up into smaller tables." Several of these modules had been pulled to opposite corners of the large space. Teams from different parts of the company were huddled together. Some were listening to music, everyone on headphones, evidently moving in time to the same rhythm. Some were assembling samples of music and speech into collages of meaning, shaping a project through a process that's more sculptural than linear.

In the kitchen, four people were quietly constructing arrangements of food from the raw and cooked ingredients on hand. They were working on a new food product, challenging themselves to assemble its essence on plate, handing each other edible messages to experience, discuss, and interpret.

Through a doorway at the far end I could see into an adjacent room. There, team members were performing a scene depicting an impasse they'd been facing. Over the next hour or so, Sandra told me, they'll act out half a dozen different resolutions, trying them on for size.

"If you've worked at the company for a year or more, you've already spent at least two weeks in various settings—theaters, music studios, dance studios—for arts-based learning," Will told me, "in addition to your design lab experience in the normal course of work. Going back to 2014, at every Fortunato office, our initiation in the new paradigm began with a week of immersion learning for every employee, starting with senior leadership. Everyone gets another week of immersion each year independent of any project they might be working on—a refresher course, so to speak."

Back in his office, I asked Will if everyone had an easy time making the transition to a design-lab culture.

"Of course not," he laughed. "Some of the senior people thought the whole thing was a joke. But not for long. I want you to talk with Dick Miller, one of the old-line Fortunato people who's really embraced the new organizational culture." Will went back to the intercom, and it wasn't long before we were joined by someone who did look a lot more like my mental image of a corporate CEO. "Dick Miller," Will said, "Rebecca Price, the journalist I mentioned. She wants to hear about the transition."

Dick laughed. "Will has already told you he had to drag me kicking and screaming, right?"

I smiled.

"That first immersion was like a trip to Mars," Dick said. "They took us out to this retreat center and divided us up into groups. Each group got a team of artist-facilitators, and they pulsed us through a sequence of action-learning—this is all language I know now, you understand, but then, it was Greek to me. They told us the idea was to use many different art forms to discover our own senses and feelings, to heighten our awareness, develop our expressive capacities, and reflect on our experience. That sounded like a load of crap to my old ears. It was like I'd stepped through the looking-glass into the 'anti-business'— everything they wanted us to do, we knew it wasn't really okay in the office environment.

"So, yes, we were suspicious. Was it some kind of trick? Some kind of elimination round for the old and un-hip? We really didn't know what we were supposed to do. If Will hadn't stood up and made an impassioned speech in which he ticked off every one of our hidden-agenda fears, I think a bunch of us would have just gone through the motions. Will promised that this was not some kind of performance assessment: no one was going to be fired or promoted or anything based on what they did here. But if we entered in, we would learn things that would definitely help our performance back at the office. He put it in terms of integration, synergies, executing the culture; we'd heard those things before. The guy has an honest face." Dick looked at Will, who smiled and shrugged. "We believed him, so we loosened up to the best of our ability and took a chance.

"It's been seven years, but I remember it like yesterday. In the first exercise, a team of jazz musicians led us through a series of listening and music-making experiences. The idea was to teach the art of improvisation: when to lead and when to listen, how to collaborate, how to have a conversation without words. The essence of that art form, they told us, is to access 'freedom within chosen constraints.' I really like that phrase. I still use it all the time.

"Out of that whole week, my favorite thing was the story-circles. We each shared a story about one of the first songs we listened to again and again, what it meant to us, why it gripped us. The tune that popped into my mind was 'You've Really Got A Hold On Me,' by the Miracles." Dick laughed. "Have you even heard of that? You're looking at me like 'What is this codger going on about? Rock'n'roll, really?' But I was young once, just like you.

"As a kid of 14, I could tell the song was about desire and power, but life hadn't yet prepared me to understand the feelings it triggered.

It was exciting and mysterious. And addictive. The facilitator called it 'an able vehicle for expressing the power of music in young people's lives.' I suppose so: I remembered lying for hours on my bed, gripped by something in that song that seemed to fill an empty place with a promise of things to come. I couldn't have said any of that, of course. I just knew I had to play it over and over again.

"Everyone there had some song like that. They were all different, and it was an amazing experience to catch a glimpse of each person in terms of his or her younger self, through music. When people told about their songs, it was like watching them travel back in time.

"We also had an experience with Forum Theater. I learned a lot more about that later with Sandra in the design lab. It's like a rehearsal for life. We use it all the time now: we create a scene that captures some challenge we are facing. It could be a project—how to package or brand something, maybe—or some difficulty in connecting between divisions or with clients. We trade off playing the key roles until we've tried out every solution we can think of. We almost always find a way to dissolve some stalemate or break our ideas out of their box, come up with something surprising.

"Now that I start talking about it, there's so much more. I can't believe how much we learned from creating self-portraits: there were props and backdrops we could use to pose ourselves so that the photo told a story. By that time, we were sort of warmed up. The self-portraits focused on our feelings about the creative risk involved in this big cultural change. We each came up with a caption for our portrait. The funny thing was, they were all so different yet each one seemed deeply true. Many of them were surprising. That exercise really changed the way our coworkers saw us. Everybody who's done it refers to that experience all the time: what we know about someone from the outside—age, appearance, race, gender, all the demographic details—doesn't necessarily mesh with how that person sees him or herself. But it's the self-identity we relate to, not the labels.

"Those first few days, we plunged into a dozen different ways of self-exploration and self-education. It was fun and challenging. We learned through direct experience, and then we were led to learn more by reflecting on our experience. And that was a revelation, you know? Time for reflection in the workplace? You've got to be kidding!

"The whole thing seemed kind of magical. Unprecedented. I thought about it a lot afterwards. How did that work? I realized that every session did two things. Each one showed us something about our own ability to take in information, and also what we'd been missing. The facilitators kept talking about bodies, feelings, and spirits. At first, that made no sense. But after a day or so, we felt like some kind of veil had been pulled back. Colors, textures, and shapes that we hadn't seen before came into focus—you know how things show up in black light? It was like that. Stuff we looked at all the time but didn't really see, that became visible. And somehow, that shattered all these stale assumptions and old habits that helped to keep things stuck at work. And that was the proof of the whole thing, that new ideas began flowing from the first day. Really, they've never stopped."

"So you spent a week at this," I asked, "and everything shifted?"

Dick chuckled. "I probably sound like a true believer, but let me try to explain. It isn't that a few days here and there instantly transformed our company's culture. From the first moment we stepped back into the office—especially in the early days, when we came back into projects and meetings with colleagues who hadn't been with us—there was a powerful magnetic pull toward the old ways. For many people, the fear was that this would be a time sink: 'In addition to keeping the numbers up, now I have to *collaborate* with everybody? Now I have to be *arty*?'

"It took work to convince people that this would actually free them from the numbers, that collaborating when it made sense would give them more alone creative time when they needed that. Sometimes, I swear it felt like trying to run in deep water or quicksand. We had to be willing to let ourselves feel foolish by saying or doing things that were taboo in the old culture. Will and his people were smart about that: they told us this was coming. They told us what to expect. Part of our training was to prepare for how it would feel when old habits and old pressures reasserted themselves.

"Something that really cinched it for me," Dick said, "was seeing how other people responded. Back when the conference room was still the conference room and not the design lab, one of our colleagues always seemed only halfway present, like the person at a reception who keeps looking over your shoulder for someone better to network with. So, about a year after the first immersion experience, he came to my office. He told me 'Work is still work, Dick, but it's also play, and the results are so much better than I ever imagined.' He said, 'Sometimes I think I'm dreaming, but if I am, I don't want to wake up.' Once I heard that from this guy, I knew it was real. I never looked back."

CATCHING THE WAVE,
CONTINUED
2033

The final part of "Chronicles" was the most fun to write. I turned everyone loose and recorded their conversation. They're all smart and opinionated and observant—and talky—so the only challenge was editing it down. I've already mentioned that Dan Kahn and I had become friends after the piece appeared. Anya Greenberg didn't enter the text till the final section, but she had a big influence. We still visit from time to time too. I think of her as the grandmother I wish I'd had. She doesn't like to tell her age, but she must be around 85. She's slowed down, but not as much as one might imagine.

In "Chronicles," I described her as "relentless," which still seems accurate and occasionally, exhausting. She's more than twice my age—I turned 40 last year, which seemed less momentous when I thought about Anya—but sometimes I have to ask her to pause the flow of words, just so I can take a breath and assimilate. On this occasion, though, the relentlessness wasn't hers alone. What made the conversation so interesting is that all of the participants shared that quality. Each, in his or her own way, had seen something emergent, and all, in their various ways, felt impelled to say what they'd seen—and to keep on saying it until everyone listened. Anya likes to quote the philosopher Ken Wilber about paradigm shift. "More depth, less span," she says, meaning that when a new way of understanding the world emerges, a relatively small number of people get it, but they *really* get it. And if they really get, they usually want to talk about it.

When The Wave started to take shape, many scientific analyses of social phenomena were in play: vector analysis, tipping points, viral memes, the 80/20 rule. However we may label it, the people I interviewed were part of the 20 percent, something like the equivalent of early adopters of a new technology. Nothing devised by human beings is perfect, of course, and none of them seemed much inclined to serene satisfaction with what they'd wrought. But along with their criticisms of the way The Wave may have failed to reach its full potential, there's a shared sense of fulfillment or gratification. I think it comes from having lived through a period when the fate of civil society seemed in doubt, then emerging into a more congenial time, when the worst evils they denounced are in decline, when the chief values they espoused continue to ascend.

That describes me too, I suppose. One good thing about looking back in 2033 at what I wrote a decade earlier is that just about everything that seemed tenuous or fragile in 2023 is stronger now. If things had turned out differently, my assignment could have been to reconsider the over-optimistic fantasies of a young writer. I could be writing now to say just how very wrong I was.

When I told Anya about this assignment, that's what she said about the sixties: that she and her cohort had been deluded, believing that ordinary Americans shared their values and aspirations. They got their hopes way up, and some of them never recovered from the tumble into disappointment. That helped me see what she meant when she said how lucky it was that I'm not in the same pickle. But of course, the way things have turned out so far makes her lucky too. She just had to wait a few decades longer for her luck to kick in.

I'm not foolish enough to predict the future. The world turns, and things can happen that beggar imagination. But when I look back, I see that once they are rooted in human cultures, certain changes tend to endure. Yes, it took a long time for the emancipation of women to spread around the globe, but the direction—the prevailing wind—was always emancipatory, despite setbacks. There was never a real possibility that the great mass of women who had access to education and livelihood would voluntarily surrender their rights; and because women make up half the world, despite intense pressure in that direction, there was never any real possibility that women as a class would be forced permanently backwards. It look a long time for a thirst for democracy to swell enough to impel the protests and revolutions they called the "Arab Spring," but once North Africans had access to multidirectional communications, once they had means of acting together that couldn't be fully quashed by suppressive centralized authorities, the dance might have been two steps forward/one step back, but the overall direction was toward freedom.

If I were inclined to bet, I'd put my money on the side that says the wind that brought us The Wave will continue to blow.

CHRONICLES OF THE WAVE
PART 4: THE GREAT CONVERSATION
2023

"That's a Wednesday," Anya Greenberg messaged me, "so I'll meet you at the Union Square Greenmarket at 1:30, southwest corner of 14th."

I hadn't been standing there for more than a minute when a smiling, animated woman ran straight at me, white hair flying, calling out at the top of her voice: "Glorious, isn't it? And this is the 56th year! I'd say this all started in 1976 with the greenmarkets. But then I'd have to contradict myself: it was the sixties with the women's movement, the civil rights movement. It was all the things that opened new doors and brought new people inside."

So far, every conversation I'd had with Anya seemed to start *in medias res*. My impression is that she'd been involved in one continuous conversation for decades, maybe a lifetime. Many people had taken part in shaping The Wave, or at least making it possible for people to see it take shape: articulating the underlying ideas, pointing out how things were changing (and sometimes, how they weren't changing fast enough: as the poet Randall Jarrell wrote, "The people who live in a Golden Age usually go around complaining how yellow everything looks"). What distinguished Anya was her relentlessness: she'd seen it early, she seen it clearly, and she'd been writing, speaking, and cajoling about it ever since. Since I was interviewing so many specialists for this series, I thought it was important to talk with someone whose stock-in-trade was the overview. Anya was happy to oblige. This was our third meeting.

"The greenmarkets?" I asked. "Why the greenmarkets?"

"Well, think about it." Twisting the white hair into a knot, she tucked it into the straw hat that had been flapping in her left hand. "In the old paradigm, food is a factory product. Each item is a single unit in a huge product array. None of them has a story or a deeper meaning, unless you count some bizarre product-development saga, Colonel Sanders' secret recipe or something—do you remember that?" She glanced at me, then carried on without waiting for a reply. "But here in the Greenmarket, each apple has its own story: who grew it, where and how? How is it best eaten, raw or cooked? What is its place in a local culture's iconography? In the cooking of different cultures? People wanted to eat food that was grown by named individuals, who in turn wanted to connect with those who ate and appreciated the fruits of their labor. New pleasures opened up: the sight of the summer's first tomatoes or peaches. The scents, the textures. Instead of food shopping being a necessary evil, it becomes a story: *Guess what I saw at the farmer's market today?* Slow food instead of fast. You are what you eat. Rage against the machine."

Seeing my puzzled expression, Anya laughed. "Sorry," she said, "I tend to get carried away."

We were headed uptown for a group conversation with key people I'd interviewed for this series. After I'd explained what I was doing with the story, Anya pointed out that it was all very specific—how The Wave changed education, commerce, medicine. She said that it was also important to pay attention to the texture of life, the little things that add up to our subjective, everyday experience. She suggested meeting earlier and meandering through a couple of neighborhoods together, talking about what we saw.

Now she leaned in, confidingly, her voice almost at a whisper. "You're fulfilling one of my fantasies, you know."

I raised my eyebrows attentively.

"I always aspired to be Jane Jacobs, who learned so much worth knowing from walking the city's streets." Anya paused, thinking. "Maybe that's when it all actually started, *The Death and Life of Great American Cities*, 1961. Sixty years ago."

"People keep suggesting The Wave started long ago and far away," I said. "Of course, there's nothing new under the sun and all that. There's always been this countervailing tendency—in college my professor talked about the Arts and Crafts Movement versus the Industrial Revolution, etcetera. The relevant thoughts probably started at the dawn of time. But I'm choosing to mark the turning point where large social institutions and whole sectors of the marketplace began adopting different cultures and organizing principles. I'd say the big shift was from a dominant way of being that had its critics—sometimes a lot of them—to a massive change in outlook and behavior. And if you look at it that way, it's the last decade that has been the most significant. The other side of the tipping point."

"Interesting. Arguable, highly arguable, but interesting. Anyway," she smiled, "we're taking a little tour of the present moment, on that we can agree, no?"

I nodded, and we set out. In just under two hours, We criss-crossed the island, the West Village to the East, Kips Bay to Gramercy Park to Chelsea, Turtle Bay to Times Square to Hell's Kitchen. For Anya—I suppose for anyone who has been paying attention for a long time—the city is a palimpsest, a drawing erased and redrawn countless times. Under the surface of 2023, she sees 2013, 2003, all the way back to the 1960s, and that reveals changes that aren't immediately evident to a less experienced eye.

We stood at Madison and 23rd, gazing at the latest public art installation in Madison Square Park. A sculptor had planted a temporary garden of the oldest plants native to Manhattan Island, cloned from seeds unearthed in archeological digs. A graceful stop-motion film was projected onto diaphanous scrims anchored in the trees, showing a loop of the plants' growth process from seed to sprout to full flower and back to seed, repeating over and over again with a reassuring rhythm.

"Look at those guides," Anya said, pointing here and there toward figures in leaf-green uniforms. "Madison Square—every park, nowadays—has a visible presence of people who are there to clean up, answer questions, give directions. Look over there, by the kiosk."

A young woman in one of the green uniforms stood next to a kiosk labeled with the name of the exhibit. You could choose one of several screens to watch: a demonstration of how these native plants were used in indigenous people's cooking, or an overview of the geologic and natural history of this land. The young woman was deep in conversation with a visitor.

"Today, there's this highly visible presence of guides and caretakers in New York. In every city, you know, not just here. You don't have to interact with them; they don't accost you or get in your way, but they're there if you need them. Nowadays we are used to the idea that it is someone's job to take care of our parks and streets, to assist visitors, to look after things. But that wasn't always so. When I was young, the only real public presence was the police, stationed here and there to keep order, and street-sweepers who nobody talked to. And later on, the homeless, who were ignored too. To walk our streets and not see beggars, not see able-bodied men using the gutters as toilets and women huddled under heaps of old coats and blankets using torn-open cardboard boxes for beds, that tells me things have changed. But I digress—always, my dear, forgive me.

"Police are still part of every city too, of course. But now, in addition to the blue-uniforms keeping an eye out for problems, there's the welcoming green presence of the Guide Corps. I understand it's the number-one choice of young people who want to do some kind of community service. Why not? It's fun and interesting. If you're in the Guide Corps, you learn a lot about the city, you meet all kinds of people, and your interactions are overwhelmingly positive, which is quite a change from the way people used to tighten up when they saw a cop or soldier."

Anya gestured expansively with an extended arm, taking in perhaps a dozen guides. "All this is grounded in a basic change in our idea of work. The old-paradigm idea was that we should replace as many jobs as possible with automated systems. That gave way to a full-employment model grounded in providing public goods like conviviality, safety, transparency, and interpersonal connection. Back in the early teens, it seemed that society could never pay for these social goods. A lot of people thought it was too far-fetched to even imagine: invest in *conviviality?* Give me a break! But once enough people understood that we could redeploy the excess we'd been spending on war, incarceration, and tax breaks for the top bracket—and that the public-service jobs we could create with those funds would boost the economy by putting money into circulation for rent and groceries and all sorts of goods and services—it started to seem obvious. And that's how things change, right? It's like childbirth: You push and you push and suddenly, something gives way and you don't have to push anymore."

A notice-board at the park entrance said that the next installation, beginning in a month, would decorate the park as the site of a Hindu wedding, with projections and spectacles in honor of Diwali, the approaching festival of lights. There would be musical concerts, and a Kathakali performance based on the tale of Romeo and Juliet.

"Did you know," Anya asked, "that this piece of earth has been a potter's field, an army arsenal, and a refuge for juvenile offenders? And all that was after European settlement and before the 19th century was half over. The first baseball team practiced here too."

I told her yes, that I'd heard at least some of that, because I loved the "whisper" network that had been threaded through much of Manhattan in the last few years. You could stand at almost any location in the city and use your own phone or smart glasses to browse through a wealth of downloadable stories that shared the history of that particular place. Some were oral history recordings—first-person stories collected by historians and artists—and others were retrievable as newspaper facsimiles, old tintypes, early video footage. Anya loved it too. When we reached Hell's Kitchen, we stood on the corner of 9th and 46th, leaning toward each other, listening on our own phones first to an archival recording of an ancient Irish voice recounting a boy's last street-fight on that corner, and then watching as the actress Ellen Burstyn talked about sharing an apartment there with another student at the nearby Actor's Studio, about never dreaming that eventually she'd become its codirector.

"The city's infinite layers are visible now," Anya said, "its infinite richness. Now we have a choice. You can still walk along in anonymity, lost in your own music or thoughts. But you are aware how many ways there are to connect with the other human beings, past and present, who have created community here. There used to be a law of the jungle in big cities. Maybe a plaque would mark the former presence of an important person or institution. But the lives of those who'd passed through without acquiring wealth or position, just working and caring for their families and making their way day-to-day, they were swept aside like dust.

"Now we're all here, all the natives and all the waves of immigrants, taking our turns, making our presence known. Back in the day, public spaces were filled with general-on-horseback statues—or the modern equivalent. The idea was to edify the public by bringing us into proximity of Great Men or Great Art. Now, the underlying idea is very different. It's that public space reflects the immense collaboration that makes a city, all those who pass through, all those who leave something behind. These changing exhibits, these sound installations, all the varieties of public memory we now take for granted, are part of a conversation between the future and past that invites everyone to participate. And so many more of us have an active stake in civic life because of it. So that's your Wave—no, dear?"

Without waiting for my reply, Anya paused to read something in a shop-window. "Look at this, 'Legislative Theater in Greeley Square.' I'm sure you know this, don't you?"

I told Anya that I'd heard quite a bit about Augusto Boal, especially from Lulu and Jacob. I recited what I knew. He'd been a Brazilian theater director, organizer, and theorist of drama in the service of democracy. Boal invented something called "Theater of The Oppressed," based on breaking down the invisible fourth wall between actor and spectator. He coined the term "spectactor" to describe a role that moves from audience member to actor and back. He used theater not merely to entertain, but to explore real-life problems and solutions. By the turn of the millennium, Boal's work had thousands of practitioners around the world.

"In the mid-1990s," Anya said, "he was elected to Rio de Janeiro's municipal legislature, and that's where he created legislative theater: People come together in a public setting for a short performance based on a proposed law or public policy. Then they use Boal's methods to try out alternative storylines. They put their heads together to imagine how the proposed measure might affect people, how to shape it for optimal effect. In Rio, all those years ago, Boal actually used legislative theater to write new laws.

"You have no idea," Anya told me, "how deadly public hearings were in the old days. Politicians and public agencies were required to give members of the public an opportunity to speak their minds about things that might affect them. But mostly, their hearts weren't in it. There would be these interminable nights where the people who cared about an issue lined up for hours to get one or two minutes apiece to address the Borough Council, for instance. It was so disheartening: most Council members didn't even pretend to listen. The meta-message of the whole enterprise was to remind us that the heart of democracy was missing. You could see people steeling themselves to do it anyway, just because they couldn't bear to keep silent."

"And now every Council member uses these artistic technologies," I said. "I have a friend who's been posting digital stories to a Manhattan Borough site exploring the future of the High Line. He's convinced it's the perfect place for an intensive garden that recycles gray water as a model for urban farming. He's made these brilliant clips stating his case. They're getting a lot of attention."

"That's what I mean by the texture of life," Anya explained. "We see a notice for legislative theater, and it opens a conversation about how political life, civic dialogue, has changed through this thing you're calling The Wave. We can look around us and pick almost anything and that thread will lead to a noticeable change. Go ahead, dear," she said, "try anything, just random."

I pointed to a young man sipping coffee at a sidewalk table, bent over a smallish rectangle of ePaper.

"He's reading, of course," said Anya. "But look how his foot is moving in time, a regular beat. Let's move closer." She peered over his shoulder. "Just as I thought. He's using the soundtrack option. Epublications didn't even have that until the late teens, as you know. It seems so obvious now, that certain writers, for certain subjects, would want to provide music and other sounds that deepen and extend the impact of their words. It seems so obvious that we take in information in different ways—that to understand deeply, some of us need an auditory or kinesthetic or olfactory dimension as well as a cognitive one. But it wasn't the least bit obvious to most people until The Wave took shape."

We'd reached our destination. Part of Zeitgeist.com's lobby was screened off by translucent walls reminiscent of shoji screens. "Let's stop for a minute before we go up," Anya said. "I love these walled gardens."

"Walled gardens" has become the popular term for the interior spaces dedicated in recent years to respite, just as the new outdoor resting spaces have been dubbed "parklets." In most buildings, walled gardens adjoined public restrooms, two types of respite. (Anya pointed out how grotesque it had been even a decade back, when the default assumption was that people would have to pay—at least indirectly, by buying a cup of coffee or something—for the privilege of using the toilet.) The walled gardens had soft light, comfortable seating, and almost always, a planting of fragrant blooms. There was a water fountain and a bank of charging stations. A green-uniformed guide was stationed outside the door to this walled garden, ready to greet visitors and answer questions. It was okay to talk quietly, a sign said, but no loud voices or music.

"Aaaah," said Anya, sinking into a chair. "To me, these are the essence of the new reality. When I think what it took for us to recognize that humans need respite! When I think about the pace we used to keep, about the way we were expected to ignore body, emotions, spirit—everything except maximum productivity with maximum efficiency—without counting the costs to ourselves!" She shook her head. "It seems so crazy now, I can hardly believe it."

Half an hour later, we were in Zeitgeist.com's meeting-room. It wasn't as fancy as Fortunato's design lab, but there was a family resemblance: markers, paints, papers, glue, scissors, 3-D printer, ePaper printer, touch screens. Come to think of it, there was also a family resemblance to the classrooms at Lisa Yoon's school—and there stood Lisa, gazing out the window, a cup of coffee in her hands. Dan Kahn was talking animatedly with Will Ford. Lulu and Jacob were off in a corner, heads together, whispering and smiling. I greeted everyone and invited them all to sit down.

As people moved toward the table, I collected some poster board and supplies from the shelves, plopping them onto the center of the table, which was already piled with old magazines. "If you want to play while we talk," I said, "be my guest. I had an idea that we could do collage depictions of The Wave."

"Vision boards!" exclaimed Anya. "I used to do them with my women's group every year: create an image of what you want to manifest in the coming year, and keep it around as a focal point and reminder. The thing is, I don't know if the boards ever helped create the future, but we had the best talks while we were busy with our hands and scissors and glue. Making something with your hands frees the mind, as women have always known—sewing together, cooking together. But of course, back in the day it wasn't knowledge till it was scientifically validated."

"Let's start by going round for introductions," I suggested. "Say a little about who you are and anything that comes to mind about The Wave, just a minute or so apiece to start us off."

"Dan Kahn, Dr. Feelgood's." Dan raised his cup in a little salute. "What you said," he glanced inquiringly at Anya, who mouthed her name, "Anya Greenberg." Dan looked surprised, made a little bow with his head, raised his cup a few inches higher. "Anya," he continued, "what you said made me think of my first wife Nikki, who passed away in 2009. I'd have to google what year it was when this happened, but right after I first met her, she was outraged at some expensive study that was supposed to provide scientific validation for the proposition that mother's milk was good for babies. When the need for that type of validation for the obvious came to an end—that's what Nikki thought would prove that times have changed, when the things people know in their cells, through their bodies and lived experience, would be accepted as valid knowledge on a par with formal, data-based studies."

On Dan's left, Jacob shook his head. "Jacob Oumarou, New York now, Burkina Faso once upon a time. I work with a company called Witness for Youth that makes theater with refugee kids. The world still makes too many refugees, and Africa is still waiting for indigenous knowledge to be given full value. I do not think The Wave has rolled all the way across that continent yet, but it is making headway, I give you that."

"Lulu Francis." Her face serious, Lulu sat up straighter, swiveling to meet the eyes of each person at the table. "I'm part of the storyteller corps at Bellevue Hospital. I'm also an environmental and social justice activist. And I have some questions about what Rebecca calls 'The Wave,' mostly having to do with whether it's a social movement or a marketing ploy. Is it just for people who can afford to shop at Dr. Feelgood's?"

Dan tilted his head to one side and brought it back upright, almost as if he were shaking water from his ear. Then he shrugged.

"Hello, everyone. I'm Guillermo Ford. You can call me Will." Will smiled. "I'm CEO of Fortunato, a global design firm." He looked at Lulu. "A lot of people who can easily shop at Dr. Feelgood's can't afford our services, so I might be the biggest capitalist villain here. But I'm also an immigrant from Puerto Rico, the first in my family to attend college—a poster-boy for upward mobility, yes? And I started a pro bono project at Fortunato applying our design skills to repurposing the large number of maximum security dinosaur carcasses left over from the prison-building boom of twenty and thirty years ago—gutting them and making them into schools and respites and clinics. Things do change. Our friend

Rebecca"—he smiled in my direction—"calls it 'The Wave.' I think I see what she's talking about, but I want to hear how all of you see it before I make up my mind." Picking up a colored marker, Will turned to Anya, who was bent over a page torn from a magazine, cutting out a photo of a farmers' market, a cornucopia of fruits spilling across a long plank table.

"Anya," I said. "You're next."

She looked up, slightly startled. "Sorry, dear. Sorry. I just love this stuff. C'mon, you should all try it. Just cut things out that resonate somehow with your idea of The Wave, and then glue them down in whatever arrangement you want. All of our boards will be different, but I bet they will be the same in some ways too."

Dan reached for a pair of scissors, Will for a travel magazine.

"I'm Anya Greenberg," she said. "Freelance troublemaker, paradigm-shifter, writer, speaker, you-name-it. I used to say I was a sixties person in both meanings—the era and the age. But now I've outlived the second meaning. And I'm glad I lived to see so much of what I've envisioned since the sixties come to life. Of course, it's nothing like we imagined it, and yet, it's exactly the same: more color, freedom, movement. Flow." She smiled and sighed.

"My name is Lisa Yoon, and I'm the principal of P.S. 124, Yung Wing School in Chinatown." Lisa laughed. "I spend a lot of my time surrounded by scissors and glue, but I don't get to play with them all that much." She reached for a piece of poster board. "School has changed, I'll say that. Some of you must have kids."

Will raised his hand, three fingers showing. "Two girls and a boy. They're with me half-time."

"Grandkids," said Anya.

"Step-kids," said Dan, "but too old for school."

"I was bored to death through school," said Lisa. "Multiple-choice tests on a computer, memorizing questions and answers for weeks before the big standardized tests, pop quizzes. I can't remember the last time I heard a student complain of boredom at our school. Whatever label you want to slap on it, things have changed."

"And I'm Rebecca, of course, and I'm really grateful to all of you for taking time for this conversation." I brandished a pair of scissors. "Most of the questions I've been engaging for this series don't have definitive answers, or at least not any that I've found." I pointed to my poster board, where a half-dozen cut-outs were loosely arrayed. "I'm going to make my Wave in the shape of an infinity symbol—you know, a sideways figure eight. No hierarchies.

"I'd like us to start with a few big questions that have emerged from our interviews and conversations, and then go on to anything else that you might want to say. Okay?"

Hearing no objections, I continued. "One thing Lulu didn't mention is that she is my roommate." Lulu smiled and waved like a beauty queen, one hand swiveling gracefully. "So we've had lots of time to talk about all this, usually late at night. Lulu can speak for herself, of course, but as she's already pointed out, she's raised the question of whether this is just another luxury masquerading as social change. She compared it to the Prius a couple of decades ago. What do you think?"

Lisa was the first to speak. "I don't think any social phenomenon has just one meaning. Yes, the Prius was a way for people with money to feel better about driving. It also cut carbon emissions. The fact that everyone couldn't afford one didn't cancel the fact that it was an improvement over gas-guzzlers. It paved the way for hybrid cars, electric cars, hydrogen-fueled cars, and much better car-sharing and public transit. It was both, a luxury and a harbinger."

"'The perfect is the enemy of the good,'" said Anya. "If I had a dollar for every time I've quoted Voltaire on that one, I'd be a rich woman, my dears. That was a kind of left-wing malady when I was young: reject everything that fails to meet your standards of perfection, and always be harder on anything that tries."

"That's not fair!" said Lulu. "Pretending to do good when you're only exploiting an issue for profit can be worse, because you're fooling people into thinking they're making things better."

"That's a tough question," Anya replied. "What are you measuring? If you're measuring actual carbon footprint, then reducing it a little is better than not reducing it at all. If you're measuring hypocrisy, then yes, it's more hypocritical. Hypocrisy is bad, I give you that. But no one dies of it. It's actions that kill, not attitudes."

"Attitudes lead to actions," Lulu retorted. "Let's say someone could have spent their time working for better public transit, or an end to fossil fuels, but instead that person fell for the Prius propaganda and felt all righteous about it. Those are actions, right? Actions that didn't happen and had real consequences."

"Sure," said Will. "But every time you do X instead of Y, there are consequences of some kind. What is at stake in this argument? How does it matter if Anya wins or Lulu wins?"

"Ah," said Jacob, "a realist in our midst. Everything matters to Lulu," he said, extending a hand to take one of hers, "that is who she is. But yes. This thing Rebecca is calling 'The Wave' is many things at once, I think. A luxury, a necessity. An image, a reality. Anya says it started in the sixties. When Rebecca interviewed me, I told her it started with *Négritude*, when Africans declared an identity that could stand up against the colonial drive to modernity. They saw something vital and important in our heritage, something that should not just be erased by Europe's idea of progress. That was in the 1930s. Colonized people have been resisting the imposition ever since."

"Or something like William Morris," Will interjected. "If I remember right, that's at least a hundred and thirty years ago."

"Yes," said Jacob. "Or perhaps the first mother who whispered forbidden stories to her children, so they would not forget who they were."

"What do all of those have in common?" "You're scooping up a lot of disparate things," I said. "Whatever you call it, what fits The Wave? I don't want to come out with some vague idea about a permanent counterculture. What's different here?"

"Good-bye Datastan, hello Storyland," said Anya, without looking up. She was moving a scrap of paper into place on her collage.

"That was one of Anya's first essays about what I'm calling The Wave," I told them.

"I think I read that for my oral history class," Lulu exclaimed. "Something about surfing the *Zeitgeist*, hm?"

"Mm-hmm," Anya replied. "'How to Surf The *Zeitgeist* Without Wiping Out.'" She looked up. "So you read that in school, dear?"

"Yes, yes." Lulu looked excited. "Like I said, I'm a storyteller. That had a huge influence on me. I just didn't connect it. You're *that* Anya Greenberg."

"The one and only. Small fry in a tiny pond: just an optical illusion. But I do like to think I had a little something to do with recognizing the centrality of individual story to any hope of a livable future." Anya smiled at Lulu. "So thank you for affirming that."

"No problem," said Lulu, smiling back. "Story at the center—yeah, I want to affirm that too. I mean, what I do for a living didn't really exist a decade ago. People have always told healing stories, but it was a big change to recognize narrative as a legitimate healing modality within western medicine. We're right there next to the doctors and nurses, and the respect is mutual. They see the value of our work—they're tracking the results too, so there's proof. When I stop and think about that, it feels huge, some kind of watershed moment in healthcare.

"Mostly, I'm dealing with people's physical ailments. There can be emotional roots or impacts, of course, or else the stories wouldn't matter. Jacob's work is all about healing the heart and mind with stories, and that is normal now too. But it was completely off the charts 15 or 20 years ago."

"This is all true." Jacob shook his head. "It is very good that this work is supported. And very sad that this is still needed. The planet shakes itself like a dog, and people are tossed to the corners of the earth. There is displacement, sometimes made by people and sometimes by floods or earthquakes—and sometimes it is hard to tell the difference. But things happen to us, and what we make of them depends on the story we tell ourselves. If I am hurt, do I tell myself every day that the world is a dangerous place and I can never trust again? Or do I tell myself about the miracle of survival, about my resilience and the future that awaits? When we choose our story, we make the shape of our lives. This is another thing that we have always known in some way, no? But now it seems we know it well enough to make it a foundation, and the work I do is no longer so fragile, so much in danger of evaporating."

Jacob sighed. I felt as if all of us were encompassed in his sigh. I had a feeling of unbidden well-being—grace, someone might call it—and gratitude for Jacob and Lulu in my life.

"Okay," I said. "The centrality of individual story. That's definitely one theme. And I think we have to list the other side of that coin: the end of our enchantment with data as ultimate truth, the beginning of our awareness that we were missing too much through our obsessive need to reduce everything to numbers. What else?"

"I'm not sure how to say this," said Dan, rising from his chair. "But I think I can show it." He pulled a carton from under the table and placed its contents on the table: a series of rectangular paper boxes decorated with the Dr. Feelgood's logo. He removed the first lid, revealing amber-colored diamond shapes twinkling with crystallized sugar. "This is *Kythonopasto*—Greek quince paste. The quince pulp these confections are made from is one of the byproducts of making quince jelly. Try one, they're delicious." He passed the box and people helped themselves.

"In the early teens, when the Greek economy crashed, a group of green investors put money into organic agriculture there, with the objective of complete vertical integration: grow the fruit, make the food products, manufacture the packaging—have all of the investment stay in the region to make a difference for people on the ground—with the proviso that wages and working conditions would adhere to accepted fair trade principles. Decent hours, wages, benefits, no child labor, no toxics, all the standards. But the investors wouldn't have done it if they hadn't seen a profit to be made: there wasn't any policymaker in control, just a convergence of interests and someone with the foresight to see it."

Dan looked at Lulu. "This is a luxury item. You could buy a candy bar for less, absolutely. But every sale contributes to a just, decent livelihood for Greek working people who would have been crushed in the meltdown. They would have slid into the migrant labor pool and shipped out to more prosperous parts of Europe—even though that pool was already oversupplied, already creating a major drain for migrants' home countries, major issues for the families left behind. Greece still isn't the wealthiest country; it still has serious problems. But the path has been steadily upward, and the business practices are some of the cleanest on the planet. This is what we used to call a win-win."

He opened the rest of the boxes. "This is artisanal chocolate from Madagascar, made there bean-to-bar. Green almond jellies from northern China. Walnut-pistachio halva from Iran, made with organic grape syrup. Part of The Wave has to do with social entrepreneurship, doing well while doing good. Evidently, not everyone understands or supports it," he said, glancing at Lulu. "But it's real, and it's a much larger slice of the international economy than it was even a decade ago, and it is improving lives. I can show you the numbers to prove that. *Bon appetit*." For a few minutes after he sat down, the only sounds were chewing and "Mmmmm."

"Okay," I said. "I'm going to call that an expansion and integration of social entrepreneurship and commerce. That goes on the list."

Anya looked up from her poster board. "I like that word, 'integration.' I think it goes further than data versus stories. It's much more common now to come from an integrated perspective, where we can bring our whole selves—body, emotions, mind, and spirit—to the table and be welcomed.

"This is a subtle thing," Anya continued, "and I want Dan and Will especially to tell me how they experience it, because they are the corporate guys—and Lisa, because she's dealing with school boards and regulatory agencies and so on. Back in the day, I was involved in protests and negotiations where I'd wind up in a corporate board room, sometimes the only woman at the table, and I would almost be paralyzed with the feeling that everything about me was excess to requirements. At first, I toned everything down, trying to fit in, but I still felt too loud, too soft, too much emotion, no matter what I said or did.

"Then I realized the big dissonance was because in my 'real' life, I could show up whole. All the information I was getting—if my body was picking up sensations or I was noticing certain emotions, if I felt some kind of spiritual connection coming through—most of the places I found myself, I could just say that, and people would understand. But not at a corporate meeting. Not at a hearing before elected officials. Not in the places we thought of as power spots. Of course, women weren't the only ones with feelings—that was just a stereotype. But what was the worst thing a woman could do in a board room?"

"Cry," said Lulu.

"On the nose, my dear," said Anya. "I don't imagine there's been a universal change, but from what I've seen in institutional settings, at public forums, with business leaders, there's often a lot more permission for that kind of integrated presence. You could call it the return of the body, the feelings, the spirit to the commons. And that is grounded in some type of recognition, that if we have to leave too much of who we are outside, we will not be good navigators. We just won't have all the information. Do you get what I'm saying?"

"I do," said Dan. "Because that's our business model, right? I mean, how can we base our business on awakening and attuning the senses, and then do business in the opposite way? Our Chief Virtuoso is part of all top-level meetings. People bring in food, music, readings, video clips, movement exercises—all kinds of inputs into our decisions are shared in what we call an integral way. When we think 'tools,' we think of the whole toolbox. We recognize that data isn't optimally useful until it's given a human context. Form follows function, you know?"

"Yeah, yeah." Will nodded fast. "We're still trying to get there. The design lab concept, design thinking—they are in place across the board. But there's still a barrier between whatever people see as design challenges and the rest of doing business. And I'm still trying to understand exactly where it is and how it can be moved. But I've been thinking a lot about this since Rebecca visited our shop." He nodded again in my direction, half a smile on his face. "I think there's a kind of organic movement. It feels like The Wave's value proposition has been established, and practice is catching up to that realization."

"Bureaucracy is sluggish," said Lisa. "I'm a public-sector person through and through, but the truth is, the private sector is more nimble. Public education's greatest infatuation with metrics came at the point when forward-thinking businesses had already decided that relationship was much more central to success than pursuing benchmarks. When you look at a huge social sector like education, you still see bureaucracy climbing all the way up to Congress and the policies that affect appropriations for the Department of Education. There's always this countervailing pull—still—where someone, somewhere, wants the value of our work reduced to numbers.

"So the big innovation for me—on the side of 'The Wave,' let's say—has been decentralization. I think that has to go on Rebecca's list: localism, human scale. Local schools—at the district level and in individual schools—have a lot more autonomy now that we aren't being controlled by national test-based standards. There are still standards, of course. But no one pretends that they don't involve subjectivity. We look at each child as a whole person. To assess progress, we interact with the students, we talk together about them. There's still some tension between the top-level agencies and educators on the ground, but it's not nearly as major. We can usually work things out, but even when it comes to a conflict, the feds don't always win."

"Medicine too," said Lulu. "There's a lot less paperwork with single-payer, of course. There aren't these massive agencies whose sole purpose is to reject claims. We have to justify ourselves, though. But yeah, the gatekeepers don't always win." She looked sheepish. "Truth be told, sometimes they help."

Will looked up from his poster. He'd drawn swirling wavelike shapes across the paper. "There's a common thread running through almost everything you are saying. If I were a politician, I'd call it 'full employment.' It takes more people to evaluate students' education in person than to administer a standardized test. It takes more people to have a storytelling corps at the hospital than to use the old-style intake forms and let it go at that. Dr. Feelgood's is based on personal interaction: the labor force is proportionately larger than say, the infrastructure behind the old Apple stores, where there was a certain scarcity of human interaction—several layers of computer-based insulation, long waiting times, etc.—even though we all saw it as a business with a human face. All of this is evidence that there was a shift somewhere along the line from cutting jobs to being willing to pay more people to do things that now seemed necessary. What do you call that?"

"Well, let's think about it," said Anya, staring at the ceiling. "It's a shift in priorities, right? It's a convergence of two factors, I think.

First, there was an awakening to the fact that corporations' interest in reducing jobs wasn't necessarily in the public interest. The massive unemployment of the teens—it just dragged on and on—and finally, people had enough. In the election of 2016, that was really key. The corruption scandals intensified people's disgust about public policies that enriched the wealthiest at taxpayer expense when at the same time, so many were suffering from corporations' refusal to re-invest in jobs even when their profits went up, up, up."

She shifted in her chair, shrugging. "I can't pinpoint an exact moment, but the switch was from an old story, in which we just couldn't afford things like decent healthcare, housing, and education—and if you pointed out that we could afford the planet's largest prison population and military budget, the biggest profits in history, you were accused of fomenting class warfare!" She threw her head back and laughed.

"And then there was a new story, which was, gee, we're spending all this money, why don't we spend it on the things we want, the things that benefit everyone? I think about this a lot: what changes when something seems absolutely impossible and then it's not? What makes the difference? I guess there's not a better name for it than 'tipping point.' We reached the tipping point, and things tipped." She was silent for a moment, her chin resting on one upturned palm.

"I don't know," she said. 'People power,' maybe? 'Human investment?' Or just go with 'full employment,' like Will said."

"And culture, art," said Jacob. "On your list, Rebecca. Story is one way of saying it, but I do not think that 'story' says it all. I am making theater. Dan's work is based on theater, painting, film, poetry, music—all art forms. Will is telling us that art school shaped his thinking. Lisa is telling us that her classrooms are like this, laboratories for creativity."

"Anya said it," Lulu interjected, nodding energetically. "This is a paraphrase, but I think it's close: 'Culture as the crucible in which we work out identity, shared meanings, all hope of a livable future.'"

Anya beamed. "You remember it better than I do," she said. "It's tacky to quote yourself, but the rest goes this way, I think: 'And art as the most concentrated and powerful expression of culture.'"

I turned my poster board outward, so people could see what I'd made. I'd papered the entire thing with images of oceans and waves. A swirl of little cut-outs made up the infinity sign: images of food growing and local artisans at work; groups of people leaning in to hear a storyteller; design workshops; classrooms filled with color and light—a bunch of light bulbs for bright ideas, structures made of recycled materials, whatever I could find. In the two negative spaces formed by the lobes of the sideways figure eight, I'd written two sets of words:

Design thinking

Integral awareness and empathy

Co-creation, collective leadership

Social entrepreneurship and commerce

The centrality of story

Culture as the crucible

The return of body, feelings & spirit to the commons

Decentralization

Human investment/full employment

"Okay," said Lulu. "I can't argue with any of that. But it isn't as if we now have heaven on earth. So tell me, what hasn't been swept up in The Wave? What *hasn't* changed?"

Lulu picked up her poster board, which was occupied by a central image, a funnel-shaped swirl that was a jumble of problems. At the tornado's top, Lulu had pasted a large, oval image of the Pacific gyre, far smaller than it had been in the early teens, but still a vast collection of plastic debris and particles swept into a floating island by prevailing currents. Lower down, the funnel was plastered with images of waste dumps, refugee camps, ranks of soldiers, and border checkpoints. The gaps were filled with images of white police prodding black protesters, refugee camps, tsunami survivors crowding around someone ladling soup from a huge vat, a half-dressed teenage girl on a street-corner, skin and bones except for an enormous pregnant belly.

"Racism still exists," Lulu said, dark eyes fierce. "Sexism still exists. Certain classes have privileges the rest will never approach. All the ways that human beings have been objectified in human history are with us, still. I wonder what difference The Wave makes to these people."

"Oy." That was Anya, stretching her arms above her head. "Is that the criterion, Lulu? If something doesn't eliminate every vestige of human greed, prejudice, exploitation, then it's no good at all? There's a lot that's not in human control, I think. We can't reach in and remake people's hearts. We can't magically erase whatever distortions of experience or character have made some people unable to see beyond their immediate interests. Every social movement that has tried to create something like that—what the Soviets called 'the new man'—has ended up spilling oceans of blood getting rid of the old men who didn't fit the mold, turning themselves into whatever they abhorred.

"So the question seems to be this: given human brokenness, what can we do to make things better? To a certain extent, we can control things like laws and budgets. It was better in the last century after official segregation was overturned and people of color could eat, drink, go to school with white people. More than half a century later, people move pretty easily in interracial settings, intermarriage is common, and so on. Legally mandated racism is not the issue anymore. But do people of color have to work harder in many settings for the same access and rewards? Absolutely. Are there racist gatekeepers who find ways to discriminate despite the laws? Absolutely. Is there still a funding gap in certain places between schools in low-income and wealthy neighborhoods? Are there still thousands of households where women's horizons are lower than men's? Looking around the world, are there still countless places where women's education and nutrition is even more substandard than men's? Yes, yes, yes.

"So let me ask you something, dear." Anya looked Lulu in the eye. "Since no intentional intervention or movement of any kind in the history of humanity has actually succeeded in making these fundamental changes in *all* human beings, which is better: give up trying, or do our best and take some pleasure in progress?"

"That's not a fair question," said Lulu.

"Oh, yes it is," said Lisa. "It's a real question, and everyone I know has answered it for themselves."

"I'll take door number two," said Dan.

"*Le mieux est l'ennemi du bien,*" said Jacob, laughing. "It will take a long time to correct the damage we have done before The Wave, yes? And we will never see 'the new man,' thank God. But I think that we now bring much more to the tasks that we can actually face, hm? 'The whole toolbox,' Dan said, and I agree."

"I still paint sometimes," Will offered. "Not seriously, more for pleasure or as a way of working something out. But something I learned from making art sticks with me: if you try too hard, it sucks all the oxygen out of the room. You can't necessarily *make* things happen. You have to *let* things happen. Not going passive: it's paying attention, noticing movement, and then you say, 'Wow, that's shaping up nicely." And then you get out of the way. That's the question I've been asking myself since Rebecca showed up with The Wave: how can we get out of its way? I'm beginning to see that it's as much about what we stop trying to force or control as what we start doing differently."

CATCHING THE WAVE,
CONTINUED
2033

That was Dan's cue to dig once again into his box of goodies. He pulled out a bottle of a sweetly delicious Muscat-based wine—after all these years, I still remember the taste, but not the label—and we toasted The Wave. By then, all of us were using that name more or less naturally, without the pauses and air quotes we'd needed at the beginning of our conversation.

It turned out that Dan hadn't been the only one to bring something to share. Lisa asked if we would take a few minutes to listen to some of the music her students had made that year with a resident composer. She'd equipped them with recorders and asked them to speak with their older relatives about the music of their youth, whether they'd heard it in the United States or in other home countries. The students had returned with snippets of song—lullabies, nursery rhymes, old pop songs, national anthems, hymns—all of which had been worked into a sort of oratorio which the students had then rehearsed, performed at a recital, and recorded for sale to benefit the school. As it played softly in the background, everyone else shared their poster boards.

Will's surprised us the most. Even though his opening salvo in our original interview had disarmed my stereotypical view of CEOs, I realized that I'd continue to see him as not quite real: all the trendy business vocabulary, maybe, the expensive suits. He had used markers and a brush to create a vortex of flowing colors, blue into orange into red. His board was more or less the opposite of Lulu's gyre: sucking in the gray debris of the old order and emanating a much richer, more complex collage of plants, animals, natural forms. That makes it sound programmatic, but it wasn't. Just beautiful and not so easy to parse. When I told him so, Will smiled. That time it felt personal.

We watched the sun set over nearby skyscrapers as we finished the treats Dan had supplied. People seemed reluctant to leave—we had bonded somehow, a few hours at Zeitgeist.com coming to resemble a week at summer camp.

Before we left, Anya asked if she could give a blessing. She explained that in her experience, when people are gathered, they can sometimes concentrate their intentions so that they resonate with forces at work in the world.

She joked about it. "Remember, I'm from California, so I'm allowed to do things like this. The East Coast Wave may not be quite as into the spiritual, but even here, you see hints."

"Do you know a woman called Doria?" Dan asked. "Four worlds chanting?"

"Doria, my dear! Is she still around?" Anya looked interested. "Yeah, I took a workshop with her a few years ago."

"Me too," said Dan. "Sorry for interrupting."

Anya had us stand and join hands. She invited us to close our eyes—"Only if you want to." She closed hers.

"I'm feeling the hope and caution here," said Anya, swaying slightly. "Very powerful. This is a room full of busy people, most of whom have many others depending on them. I want to express my personal gratitude to each of you for taking the time for this. But it's not just time: the open-heartedness, sincerity, willingness to learn that you have manifested today, may that be returned to each of you a hundredfold. And may that energy flow out from this group to suffuse the world, as The Wave gathers force."

I spoke to each of them again as I began work on this retrospective.

Ten years on, the doubts of 2023 had faded. Dr. Feelgood's and Fortunato are both thriving. Dan and Will have found enough excitement and challenge to remain as CEOs. If you're reading this, you may already know that Lisa Yoon is solidly ensconced as Chancellor of the New York City Department of Education and the city is better for it.

Jacob and Lulu were on vacation when we talked, visiting Burkina Faso with their daughter Coco, now nine years old. As I Skyped them, I mused that Lulu had called it correctly back in 2023—no heaven on earth is ever possible. But from her current vantage point in 2033, Lulu's skepticism had dimmed.

"I think it was the novelty of it all," she told me. "I couldn't take it in." Lulu is in academia now, the last place I would have predicted. Four or five years ago, having risen to direct the Bellevue storyteller corps, she was asked to create a new certificate program slotted under Columbia's narrative medicine degree, one that would yield a medical storyteller certification. Now she's Professor Lulu Francis-Oumarou. Things change. There were a few gray streaks in her dark curls, and a kind of composure in her posture I would not have thought possible a decade before.

"I'd been an activist all my life," Lulu said, "which kept me busy, coming up in an especially cynical period. All through high school and college, it was all demoralization, all the time. Working for Obama's election was the big thing in high school, and that didn't turn out the way we'd hoped, not at all. I was big on Occupy in the early teens, but Occupy was a rejection and refusal of the whole system. We were saying how things *should* be, but we didn't have much hope that they *would*—or even could—turn out that way. So by the time you wrote about The Wave in 2023, I had internalized the belief that systemic change wasn't really possible. I really didn't want to get my hopes up. I didn't feel able to risk the disappointment. And for a long time, I didn't really get that I was experiencing it anyway: I had pre-disappointed myself. I just skipped right over the part where you hope and try and went straight to a sort of pre-emptive failure.

"Plus, it's always a question of what you pay attention to, right? There were enough horror stories to fill my screen, if that was what I wanted to notice. Everyone was telling me the world was fucked. And I was pissed. I thought outrage equaled clarity. I wanted to stay stoked."

"So what changed that?" I asked.

Lulu chuckled. "Honestly? Mostly Jacob." Jacob stuck his head into the frame and waved. Coco popped up like a jack-in-the-box. "Hi, auntie Rebecca! I'm having fun!" I waved back.

Lulu continued. "Jacob had seen and done things I couldn't even imagine. He was working every day with kids whose lives made my juvenile experience look like a walk in the park. And still, they were generating all this possibility. It wasn't sappy. It was realistic—'Hope grounded in reality,' he used to say.

"We were in love. We were ready to get married, and Jacob sat me down for a serious talk. I thought, 'Oh-oh. He's had enough of my shit. He's going to break up with me."

Jacob's smiling face reappeared. He pointed to Lulu with one hand and make circling motions with the other: *She's nuts, isn't she?*

"Instead," Lulu continued, "He said that he loved me and he wanted us to spend our lives together, but he needed to ask me for something. He asked me to look at the protection I'd wrapped around my heart to keep from feeling disappointed. He said he didn't think his spirit could sustain a lifetime of someone he loved pouring cold water on hope every time it reared its head. He asked me how my life would be different if I didn't feel aggrieved and outraged every second of the day. He asked me how it would feel not to dismiss everything that failed to reach my standards of purity. What if I still believed in the same things, still held the same values, but just kept an open mind on whether they would prevail or not? I could do all the same things, whatever I wanted. But could I do them without holding on to the certainty that they were doomed?"

"I told her no one can know the future," said Jacob. "I told her that if someone had come to me as a boy in Burkina and said you will be in New York, making theater, about to marry a beautiful and talented American woman who loves you as much as you love her—how could I have believed a fairy tale like that? I told her she didn't have to become an optimist. But an agnostic, maybe?"

"I felt like an idiot," said Lulu. "All my verbiage about the importance of healing stories, and I'd been telling myself the same aggravating, demoralizing story for years. Jacob was right: who can know what will come? After I got through kicking myself for idiocy, I adopted agnosticism as my religion in all things."

"And we live happily ever after," yelled Coco, somewhere off-screen.

"Who knows about ever?" said Lulu. "But so far, so good. I guess you could say I caught The Wave. It's an adjustment to be happy after simmering yourself into outrage for a decade or two. Injustice still pisses me off, obviously. And of course, our work is about suffering, helping to heal it. Life is the bitter and the sweet, always. But, Rebecca, back when we were eating our ramen and scrabbling to pay the rent, if you'd told me I'd rise each morning full of gratitude for the privilege of seeing another day in which signs of awakening are everywhere, I probably would have laughed in your face and stormed out of the room.

"But here's the uncanny, crazy thing: you would have been right." Lulu shook her head, smiling. "We were on the side of history for once. It just took a while for people to notice."

ABOUT THE AUTHOR

Arlene Goldbard is a writer, speaker, consultant and cultural activist whose focus is the intersection of culture, politics and spirituality. Her blog and other writings may be downloaded from her Web site: www.arlenegoldbard.com. She was born in New York and grew up near San Francisco. Her book *New Creative Community: The Art of Cultural Development* was published by New Village Press in November 2006. She is also co-author of *Community, Culture and Globalization*, an international anthology published by the Rockefeller Foundation, *Crossroads: Reflections on the Politics of Culture*, and author of *Clarity*, a novel.

Her essays have been published in *Art in America*, *Theatre*, *Tikkun*, *Teaching Artist Journal*, and many other publications. She has addressed many academic and community audiences in the U.S. and Europe, on topics ranging from the ethics of community arts practice to the development of integral organizations. She has provided advice and counsel to hundreds of community-based organizations, independent media groups, and public and private funders and policymakers including the Rockefeller Foundation, the Independent Television Service, Appalshop, WomenArts, the Center for Digital Storytelling, and dozens of others. She serves as President of the Board of Directors of The Shalom Center.

The Wave was published simultaneously with a companion work of nonfiction on art's public purpose, *The Culture of Possibility: Art, Artists & The Future*.

Made in the USA
Charleston, SC
17 February 2014